TIMEWYRM: APOCALYPSE

THE NEW

DOCTOR WHO

ADVENTURES

TIMEWYRM: APOCALYPSE

Nigel Robinson

First published in 1991
in Great Britain by
Doctor Who Books
An imprint of Virgin Publishing
338 Ladbroke Grove
London W10 5AH

Cover illustration by Andrew Skilleter

Typeset by Type Out, London SW16
Printed and bound in Great Britain by
Cox & Wyman Ltd, Reading, Berks.

ISBN 0 426 203593

'The things around us are now no more than husks of themselves. From this point the unravelling will spread until all the universe is reduced to a uniform, levelled nothingness.

'So it's true!' the Master cried.

'Don't move. Anybody ...' The Monitor's voice came as a whisper. Instinctively they all obeyed. Even the Master stood in silence, surrounded by the creak and shuffle of surrounding structures. All eyes were on the Monitor as he continued. 'You have already guessed − our Numbers were holding the Second Law of Thermodynamics at bay. The Universe is a closed system. In any closed system entropy is bound to grow until it fills everything. The deadly secret, unknown until now beyond the bounds of Logopolis, is this ...' The Monitor's voice trembled, and they had to strain to hear his next few words. 'The fact is, the universe long ago passed the point of total collapse.'

Christopher H. Bidmead, *Doctor Who − Logopolis*

'Night is falling. Your land and mine goes down into a darkness now, and I and all the other guardians of her flame are driven from our home, up out into the wolf's jaw ... Cherish the flame till we can safely wake again. The flame is in your hands, we trust it you: our sacred demon of ungovernableness ... child, be strange: dark, true, impure and dissonant. Cherish our flame. Our dawn shall come.'

David Rudkin, *Penda's Fen*

PROLOGUE

Nothing.

Then warmth. Warm Nothingness.

Then Otherness ... Some Thing ... Something Else ... Something different ... Pulsing ... Beating ... Energies — no, lives, throbbing, pulsing, swimming around ... Feeding ...

Feeding who?

Feeding me.

Me?

Me ... me ... me ... ME!

Me.

Darkness ... And then there is light ... Bright and cold and real and shocking and painful light. Blinding me!

Calmer now. Comforting. Shadows becoming shapes. Reactions becoming reasons.

And the light shines in the darkness.

And I comprehend it!

Fifteen billion years ago there was nothing, just a cold, dark emptiness. And that void was without form or meaning.

Then there was light, a small pinprick of incalculable

1

energy which gave the cradling vacuum purpose.

Less than a millisecond passed and that superdense ball grew and shuddered, and exploded in a blazing outburst of energy and particles. They streamed out of its centre, and met and coalesced, forming new energies and atoms and molecules.

And still the detritus from that first explosion sped ever outwards, reacting and combining with each other in a marvellously ordered chaos, forming gases and new elements and solid matter.

Billions of years passed and stars were born and died in the aftermath of the great explosion. Galaxies were born, and planets created out of that first cosmic dust.

On those planets, primitive molecules formed complicated chains which, suffused with radiations, formed even greater chains to create life in all its forms from the simplest bacteria to complex reasoning beings.

Billions of years passed. Civilizations arose on those planets, and fell, and rose again. Still the Universe − for that is what those civilizations had called the aftershock of that first cataclysmic event − expanded ever outwards.

And then it stopped, the force of the explosion finally exhausted. For another billion years the Universe existed in an uneasy state of equilibrium.

On the ancient planet of Logopolis a group of mathematicians attempted to maintain that equilibrium. Through a series of complex equations they opened a series of charged vacuum emboitements − CVEs − which they hoped would stop the collapse of the Universe. Without them, they knew that the Universe would surely contract and fall back on to himself, until it finally returned to the state it was in in the beginning.

Their plans were undermined when an unthinking renegade from the legendary planet of Gallifrey upset their calculations. Logopolis was destroyed. It was only through the intervention of a mysterious traveller known to some as the Doctor that the Universe was saved.

Realizing that creation still had much to achieve, he opened a single CVE in a distant constellation. The Universe had been given a breathing space in which to prove itself.

Several more billion years passed. Civilizations arose and fell and rose again.

Then, somewhere in the region of a constellation which had once been called Cassiopeia, the CVE glimmered, blinked, and closed.

Chapter 1

'Are you afraid, my son?'

Darien nervously flicked a strand of fine blond hair out of his eyes. 'No, my lord Reptu,' he lied, 'merely confused.'

He looked around wonderingly at the sleek, stark whiteness of the room in which he found himself, and thought fondly of the finely polished marble and ornate brocades of his own home.

The old man allowed himself a smile, almost avuncular in its kindness, and his misty grey eyes sparkled.

'That is to be expected, of course. The sea voyage to Kandasi is long, and the trip disorientating even to we of the Panjistri.' He raised a hand as Darien protested. 'Though the people of Kirith regard us with awe — and rightly so — we are not so very different from you. You will learn that in your time here.'

A door slid silently open and Reptu took his hand and led him out of the room.

The change from the antechamber's stark simplicity was staggering, and Darien grabbed Reptu's hand even more tightly as he struggled to maintain his balance.

They stood on a narrow metal bridge, which with no

apparent means of support spanned a vast abyss. From the ground, thousands of feet below, huge metal towers rose from out of a misty blue glow and climbed up the opposite side a hundred feet away. Pillars of multi-coloured lights alternated with the towers, pulsing in time to the heartbeat drumming of unseen machinery.

At intervals on the towers there appeared a stylized skull design, the macabre badge of the Panjistri. The air was tangy with some heady incense and through the skylights in the huge domed ceiling Darien could see the stars in the night sky.

Behind the windows of the towers Darien saw members of the Panjistri, the supreme guardians of Kirith. They were dressed in their customary habits and skullcaps, some scarlet like Reptu's, others of different colours which denoted their lesser rank. Each of them went about his or her silent and secret business and paid no attention to the two newcomers. Curiosity was a mortal failing and the Panjistri were far more than mere mortals.

'Kandasi, the wonder of the world,' explained Reptu matter of factly and added, 'It's better if you don't look down.' Pulling Darien behind him he marched off briskly over the bridge, seemingly unconcerned by the lack of any handrail along the structure.

'You lied earlier when you denied being afraid,' said Reptu without any hint of reproach. 'But fear, like mediocrity, has no place here. As we cross this bridge over the abyss, so we walk the tightrope to our destiny. And our destiny is to recognize our highest potential and then surpass it. What have you done to surpass your potential, Darien?'

'My lord? I don't understand,' he said, fervently hoping that all the Panjistri didn't talk in such riddles.

A note of impatience entered Reptu's voice, shattering his air of cold serenity. 'On Kandasi each of us has made

5

his or her way from the burrowing worm to the sentient beings we now are. We are chosen, special and unique, the seed of the lightning flash. Each of us has his own special talent. That is why we are chosen. Tell me what you have to offer the Brotherhood of Kandasi.'

'I have some little skill with music, sir,' Darien admitted, and kicked himself as he realized that Reptu would see through the false modesty as easily as he had through the earlier show of bravado.

Darien had, in fact, been a child prodigy. At the age of five he was already master of the *koríntol*, the traditional wind and string instrument of the Kirithons, with its 470 keys and a sound which, it was said, could bring the stars back to the night sky. The next year he was performing his own compositions in public: it was said that one of his recitals had even moved the dark and saturnine Lord Procurator Huldah, leader of the Brethren, to tears!

Now at sixteen he was one of the most respected and popular musicians in his town. His decision to join the famed Brotherhood of Kandasi to practise and refine his art had provoked muted protest from many quarters. But as Lord Huldah had pointed out, it was the greatest honour which could ever be accorded a Kirithon.

It was not an honour accepted hastily. When members of the Brethren first approached his parents four years ago, Darien refused. He had no wish to spend the next ten years of his life with the old men and women on Kandasi Island, even for the sake of his music; the only decent conversation he'd get there would probably be from the sheep. His parents were also reluctant for their only son to leave home quite so soon.

Only his older sister seemed keen on the idea. He would bring shame on the family if he refused, it was a tremendous honour, a marvellous opportunity to become the greatest musician and composer of the age, she only wished she had his talent . . . As Revna had about as much appreciation of music as a dead dung beetle, Darien suspected the real reason for her enthusiasm was to get him out of the way and become her parents' favoured child again.

When his father died suddenly in a boating accident, things changed. The Lord Huldah himself (how that impressed the neighbours!) came in person to offer his condolences and to spend more than an hour in private conversation with his mother. Shortly afterwards, his mother joined Revna in encouraging him to pursue his vocation. At the same time, audiences for his recitals were dwindling, causing him to doubt his abilities: perhaps a sojourn on Kandasi might revive his flagging skills after all. Little by little his determination was whittled away. In the end the only voice of dissent was that of his best friend, Raphael; and as his musical talents were even less than Revna's (Darien had never quite forgiven him for once falling noisily asleep during a concert) Darien decided that Raphael really didn't know what he was talking about.

And so, after some initial instruction from Huldah, Darien had set out for the Harbours of the Chosen, where he was met by Reptu and taken across the seas to the Skete of Kandasi, the complex of buildings on Kandasi Island which was the home of the Panjistri.

'A musician,' repeated Reptu as they reached the other end of the bridge and entered a waiting elevator. The doors, again decorated with the skull motif, closed automatically behind them and they began their descent. 'Tell me, Darien, did you ever hear of Kareena?'

The boy shook his head and the irritating lock of hair flopped in his eyes again. He'd never heard the name before. Then he frowned. *Kareena. Kareena. Kareena.* Now that he came to think of it the name did sound familiar. He tried to remember.

'She was a dancer,' said Reptu wistfully. 'One of the greatest and most beautiful of the age. Her feet seemed never to touch the floor, and her elegance, her under-standing and empathy with the music were joys to behold. Perhaps you will write music for her.'

'She's here?' Life on Kandasi was beginning to sound better.

'Many have joined the Brotherhood,' Reptu answered. 'Artists like yourself. Scientists. Prophets. Men of great wisdom, and women of terrible vision. All part of the great venture that is Kandasi.'

He turned to look at Darien, and reached out a gnarled hand to stroke the fine down and smooth skin of the boy's round face. Darien flinched at the unwelcome attention.

'And now you are to become part of that great venture, Darien,' he said softly. 'Bear that responsibility well, for much depends on it.'

The lift came to a halt and the doors opened on to a small corridor. At the end of the passageway a pair of large imposing doors opened outwards for them, as though they were expected.

'I must leave you here while I arrange your quarters,' said Reptu. 'Make yourself comfortable and I will return shortly.'

Reptu watched the boy walk through the doors, which closed softly behind him, and sadly shook his head. Such a pity that one had to lie, he thought, and especially to the young and beautiful.

Darien entered a darkened room. The only illumination was the silvery blue glow of the moon which shone through a narrow casement. He frowned as he wondered how the sky could be seen through the window when he had assumed that Reptu had taken him miles below the Skete.

8

A shadow lurched from the half-darkness and approached him.

'Welcome, young master,' it hissed and Darien instinctively backed away.

The creature was bent almost double, but even standing upright it would only have been about five feet tall. Its snout constantly sniffed the air and its two bulbous eyes darted this way and that. Sharp, pointed ears rose on either side of the weasellish face, and when the creature spoke it revealed yellowing teeth and sharp, vicious incisors. Apart from its face, the creature's entire body was covered with thick, matted brown hair.

Darien cursed himself for his fear, knowing that the creature posed no threat to him. It was a Companion, one of those who accompanied the Panjistri on their infrequent journeys away from Kandasi, acting as the eyes and ears of their almost blind and deaf masters.

'Does Fetch disturb you?' said another, quieter voice from the shadows. 'Please, don't be alarmed. He's not as handsome as your people, but he is a loyal friend and wishes you no harm.'

'I'm sorry, I didn't mean ...'

'Oh please, don't be concerned,' said Fetch sulkily and moved away from Darien to stand at the side of the other figure, who stood silhouetted in the moonlight.

The voice was female, cracked and ancient, and at first Darien had to listen carefully to hear her. But despite its softness the voice carried a power and authority which could not be ignored. Darien peered into the darkness as the woman walked stiffly out of the shadows towards him.

The first thing he noticed about her were her eyes. Unlike the weakened eyes of the other Panjistri, hers were piercingly green and sharp; they followed his every move.

An elaborate beaded headdress framed her finely boned face. It was a face which had been beautiful hundreds of

9

years ago: now in the strange half-light it looked hollow and empty. Darien was reminded uncomfortably of the animal skulls he and Raphael had once found in the moors and highlands outside their town.

Almost seven feet tall, the old woman bore herself regally and upright despite her age and the obvious discomfort she felt in walking. One bony six-fingered hand grasped a long ebony staff, plain except for the small carved skull at its crown.

Like the other Panjistri she wore a long high-collared habit, but hers was of darkest blue and seemed to be made of a heavier and richer material; it was edged with decorative braid and glistened in the moonlight. Several slender chains of silver hung around her neck.

She smiled at Darien, revealing surprisingly white teeth. 'Welcome to Kandasi,' she said, and nodded in welcome. 'You are a musician. Please, play for me.'

Darien looked puzzled, wondering who the woman was, until he saw a beautifully crafted *korínto!* at the far end of the room.

Fetch offered him a chair, and as Darien sat the old woman came to his side, gently laying the long fingers of a bejewelled hand on his shoulder. A shiver ran through Darien's body and he looked up at the woman's smiling face. 'Now play. Play as you have never played before.'

Darien flexed his fingers and began to play. Perhaps inspired by the strange old woman, whatever doubts he had had about his skills left him and his hands glided over the keys, coaxing and cajoling hidden sounds from the instrument. The old woman stood entranced; her eyes were closed and her head nodded gently in time with Darien's playing.

All the time Fetch looked at his mistress through narrowed, questioning eyes.

With a resounding crescendo of horns and strings Darien

finished, leaned back in his chair, and sighed with self-congratulation: he hadn't played so well for a long time. He just hoped the old woman appreciated it. He looked up expectantly.

For a moment she stood there, saying nothing. Then her eyes snapped open and her mouth formed a wistful half-smile. A single tear trickled down her cheek.

'I have not heard such music for many years ... It is good that you have come to Kandasi, Darien. Now your music will fill our chambers and cloisters till the stars themselves return to the sky.'

A brief glance passed between the old woman and Fetch, who silently left the chamber.

Before Darien had a chance to wonder how the old woman knew his name, she was talking excitedly to him about his music, animatedly pointing out the nuances in his playing, the elaborate structures in his composition, his dexterity at the keyboard. He was a true genius, she gushed, in ten years' time he would surely be the greatest musician in all the Ten Galaxies.

Darien frowned and was about to ask the old woman what a galaxy was when Fetch returned. He brought with him a large crown, encrusted with jewels, its filigree streaks of gold sparkling and beckoning in the moonlight. He passed it almost reverently to the old woman.

'Be crowned our king of music, Darien,' the old woman beamed, and raised the crown over Darien's head.

Darien winced: praise was all very well, he thought, but this show of enthusiasm from a crazy old woman was becoming just a little too embarrassing. It was probably as well Raphael wasn't here. He couldn't stand ceremony at the best of times; by now he'd be howling with laughter.

The crown was placed on his head and a surge of wellbeing swept through him. In that instant his mind was opened up to all the possibilities before him — the

11

symphonies he had in him to write, the instruments he could play, the beauty he would bring into the world.

Dreamily he looked up at the passive, unsmiling face of the old woman. She was no longer the kindly gushing matron; now she was a fierce determined witch with greed and lust in her eyes.

And he was afraid.

He cried out in agony. White-hot pain seared through his body and his brain felt ready to explode. He tried to raise his arms to remove the crown, but they stayed pinned to his sides. As his flesh peeled and fell smouldering away from his face and limbs to reveal bone which instantly began to liquefy, one thought, one name ran through his mind. Not his beloved music. Not Reptu, not Raphael, not Revna.

But Kareena. *Kareena. Kareena.* The name he had never heard before.

Now he remembered.

It was the name of his twin sister.

Chapter 2

— *Wellbeing.*

Secrets half-expressed and never quite explained. And yet I understand them. I rather like that.

Contentment and harmony. Concord and unity in motion. It's pleasing to me.

Perfect, total *symmetry.*

Nonono, there is a discordance, a dissonance. Something unexpected and out of the plan.

I don't like that. It impinges upon my awareness, disturbs me with its intent of purpose. It upsets all that I comprehend.

How many dimensions can I fit into a box? How many spaces can I fit into one instant?

But then dimensions are relative. Which must mean they are all the same.

They were all the same, the scruffy little man thought grumpily, as he absently sucked the finger he'd just used for scratching his ear. Tell them one thing, and it was ten to one that they would go off and do the exact opposite. At least Ben had had the good sense to stay in the TARDIS while he stopped off to replenish his stocks of mercury.

13

But Polly, oh no, not Polly. She said that she wasn't going to be cooped up in the ship while he went off and had all the fun. You might have thought she'd have learnt her lesson by now, the little man had said. After all, their travels together had hardly been uneventful: Daleks, Cybermen, even cutthroat smugglers. Hadn't she better stay in the safety of the TARDIS and start showing a little bit of sense?

And at that she'd retorted that it was probably time that *he* started showing a little bit of sense. That had hurt. It wasn't his fault that the TARDIS's mercury supplies were seriously depleted: he could have sworn he'd stocked up several trips ago. And nor was it his fault that he noticed the lack only when they had just left a planet whose mercury swamps ensured abundant supplies of the element.

So she had stormed out of the TARDIS. She wasn't in any danger, of course. The little man knew the planet and its inhabitants well — they were a highly advanced and peaceful race, living in small communes, and tolerant of strangers. But it wouldn't do her any harm at all to see just how well she could really get along without him. So the little man had purposely taken his time renewing his stocks of mercury, and it was several hours after Polly had left the TARDIS before he began looking for her.

And of course, now that the time had come, he couldn't find her. As he walked the narrow streets of the settlement for what seemed like the hundredth time, he sulked like the little child he often pretended to be.

'Are you lost, sir?'

He looked down at the small red-headed girl tugging at his dirty frock coat. She was carrying a battered doll under one arm, and the dirty streaks around her eyes told him that she had recently been crying. There was a look of concern on her face.

'Am I lost?' he repeated, and rubbed his chin

14

thoughtfully, considering the question as he might do a complicated equation. 'Well, I don't think so. Not this time anyway.'

He crouched down beside the girl and gave her his most charming smile. She grinned back. 'But I think my friend might be lost,' he said. 'Have you seen her?'

'The tall lady with the blonde hair?' the girl offered.

'Yes, that's her,' nodded the little man. 'Her name's Polly. Do you know where she is?'

'She's over by the marketplace,' she replied, and indicated the way.

The scruffy little man thanked the girl, but as he stood up to go she tugged at his sleeve. 'Sir?' she ventured and offered him her doll.

He sat down cross-legged on the floor and examined the broken toy.

'Everything gets old and falls apart in time,' he said philosophically. 'It even happens to me.' The child's face fell until he added: 'But most things can be fixed. Let's see what I can do.'

The side of the rag doll had been ripped open and its stuffing was beginning to fall out; one eye was loose and connected to the smiling face only by a single thread.

The little man emptied one of his pockets, coming across a pair of conkers, a yo-yo, a bag of glass marbles and an old banana skin before he found the needle and thread he was looking for. With the expert hand of a tailor he set about stitching the doll together again.

His task finished, he handed the doll back to the little girl who inspected it closely and then smiled. 'Thank you, sir,' she said, and then as an afterthought: 'I like you: you're nice.'

His jade-green eyes twinkled with delight. 'And I like you, too. Would you like to hear a tune?'

The little girl nodded and he took an old, battered

recorder out of his top pocket. He warmed even more to his new friend as she clapped her hands and began to dance in time to the music he was playing. The scruffy little man smiled smugly. At least there were still people who appreciated good music, he thought: just let Ben and Polly complain about his playing again!

When he had finished, the girl smiled sadly and said: 'I must go now, sir, otherwise I'll be late for school.' She pointed to an approaching figure. 'And there's your friend now.'

The little man looked up as Polly approached. He blinked, shaking his head as his vision blurred.

The girl must be mistaken, he thought: Polly didn't have long dark hair, tied back in a braid; nor did she have a penchant for lycra leggings, an oversized leather jacket and Doc Marten boots. And Polly's voice was 1966 Rodean-vintage, while this one came very definitely from Perivale, West London, circa 1990 . . .

'Oi! Professor! Wake up! Is there anyone in there?'

The Doctor shook his head again, and his vision cleared.

He was in the main control chamber of the TARDIS, standing by the central mushroom-shaped console, his hands poised over the controls. The transparent column in the middle of the six-panelled console was slowly falling to a halt, and he found his hands skipping automatically over the instruments, guiding his time machine into a safe if somewhat shuddery landing. Then he realized that someone was tugging at his sleeve.

'Doctor, are you all right?'

The Doctor raised a hand to his forehead, and breathed deeply. 'Ace, where was I?'

His companion shrugged her shoulders. 'Dunno. One minute you're humming a Miles Davis tune, and the next you're totally out of it —'

'Out of it? How long for?'

16

'Couple of seconds, five at the most. Are you sure you're OK?'

'Yes . . . But nothing like this has happened before . . . Like a voice from my past, telling me something, reminding me . . . ' The Doctor frowned; the memory was already fading fast. 'I was looking for . . . for Polly, yes that was it. A long time ago . . .'

'Polly? Isn't that the stuck-up Sloane Ranger you told me about?' asked Ace. 'Don't worry, Professor, she'd probably only ask you for a contribution to Conservative Party funds.'

The Doctor's impish face broke into a fond smile and he chucked his companion on the chin. 'Well, she speaks very highly of you. '

'How come? I've never met her.'

'Yet.' The Doctor grinned infuriatingly and turned his attention back to the console.

His apparent good humour was for Ace's benefit. Now in his seventh incarnation, he prided himself on his level-headedness and command of the TARDIS, so different from that of his previous selves. This temporary lack of consciousness and the implication that he was losing control of things disturbed him deeply.

He activated a touch-sensitive control and looked up expectantly. The panels in front of the scanner screen remained closed. He tutted, and jabbed at the control again.

'The TARDIS is getting as absent-minded as you,' Ace said. The Doctor merely looked at her. She remembered what she had been meaning to ask him since the previous day.

'Professor,' she said. 'This is probably a silly question, but — are there any animals in the TARDIS?'

The Doctor was glaring at the scanner. 'What?' he said absently.

'Well, it's just that yesterday morning I thought I saw —'

17

'Aha!' the Doctor shouted as the panels in front of the screen slid reluctantly apart to reveal the scene outside the TARDIS.

'The planet Kirith,' he announced grandly, tapping the lapels of his brown jacket and sounding for all the world like a lecturer eager to show off to his students. 'The only planet circling a red giant in the galaxy known to you as QSO 0046, at the very edge of the explored Universe. Gravity Earth-normal, with a slightly higher oxygen and nitrogen content. Lush vegetation, few predators, and a particularly interesting native life form.'

'I'm not impressed, Professor,' said Ace. 'It still looks like a wet Wednesday in Margate out there.'

The Doctor winced. Ace did have a point, he thought, as he looked at the picture on the screen.

The TARDIS had materialized on a rocky promontory, facing on to a storm-tossed and vicious sea. Sporadic bursts of ball lightning illuminated the dark brown night sky; seabirds wheeled and turned, struggling vainly against the howling wind and rain. Huge trees on the nearby black cliffs creaked and swayed as the wind thundered through their branches.

'Well, it's still a young planet,' the Doctor said apologetically. 'The climate is bound to be a little unstable.'

Ace gave a sniff of disapproval, as though she didn't think that was a good enough excuse. As she turned back to the Doctor she missed seeing the dark silhouette of someone − something − which had been hiding behind a rock observing the appearance of the TARDIS.

'And we're not on a holiday joy ride, anyway.' There was an uncustomary note of irritation in the Doctor's voice as he drew her attention to a counter blinking steadily on the console. 'That's what we're here for.'

'The Timewyrm,' Ace whispered. 'I thought perhaps

18

she'd gone for good.'

'No such luck, I'm afraid. We've tracked her down again.'

The Doctor had saved the embryonic human civilization of Mesopotamia, on Earth, from enslavement by a mind-devouring alien creature who had set herself up as the goddess Ishtar in the city of Kish. He had had to pay a high price, however: Ishtar, already more machine than living creature, had fused with the computer virus that the Doctor had hoped would destroy her, and had then escaped into the micro-circuitry of the TARDIS. In order to prevent her taking control of the ship he imprisoned her in a section of the TARDIS that he was able to jettison into the space-time Vortex. Even this was not enough to annihilate the being that Ishtar had become. The chronovores who inhabit the Vortex named her Timewyrm, because she learnt how to use the TARDIS systems within her to slide back and forth through time.

The TARDIS, the Doctor and the Timewyrm were now indissolubly linked. The TARDIS had tracked the Timewyrm to the twentieth century on Earth, where the Doctor restored the time-lines that she had disrupted and scattered her across space and time. The Doctor had suspected that she would be able to reassemble herself, and the winking light on the console was the depressing sign that the TARDIS had detected the Timewyrm's presence and had brought them to Kirith.

'So if this Timewyrm thing is here, what do we do when we find it?' asked Ace. 'Or when it finds us . . .' she added morbidly.

'Destroy its power utterly, even at the expense of everything else, and wipe out all trace of its ever having been.' The Doctor spoke with grim determination and there was an adamantine glint in his eyes. And then abruptly, he continued in a much lighter tone. 'Anyway, I've always

19

wanted to come here. Do you know that Kirith is one of the strongest sources of artron energy in this quadrant? It's so powerful that back in the 1990s Earth astronomers mistook it for a quasar.'

'Give me a break, Professor,' Ace pleaded. 'Until a minute ago I'd never even heard of Kirith, let alone artron energy.' She sighed, hoping the Doctor wasn't going to insist she look up the relevant entries in the TARDIS's data banks. Much as she trusted and respected her mentor, there were times when his insistence that she find out things for herself reminded her a little too much of school.

'Long, long ago the Time Lords harnessed an energy force hidden deep within the mind. Channelled properly it can be used in many different ways. For instance, without it no TARDIS could function properly,' he explained airily. 'Several other highly advanced species can tap it to some degree; but why should there be so much of it on Kirith?'

'A Time Lord's stranded here and he's putting out a distress signal?' Ace suggested. 'An amoeba with delusions of grandeur is sending out a message to any intelligent life form listening in?'

'Shall we find out?' asked the Doctor and stalked over to the mahogany hatstand in the corner. He threw himself into a brown duffle coat, jauntily jammed a porkpie hat on to his mop of brown hair and propped a multi-coloured umbrella over his shoulder.

'Can't we wait till the sun comes out?'

'Time might be relative but it's not infinite,' the Doctor reproved. 'Besides, there's a town close by, we can shelter there. Doors, please, Ace.'

Ace's hand hesitated over the console before selecting the correct control. The Doctor had recently felt it was finally time that she learn some of the basic control functions of the TARDIS, and she was anxious to prove that his lessons had not been in vain. She looked up with disappointment: the double doors at the far end of the control chamber remained resolutely shut.

The Doctor raised an admonishing eyebrow. She began to protest when the doors slowly opened. The Doctor stroked his chin thoughtfully.

'Delayed reaction? Rusty hinges?' Ace suggested as she picked up her backpack from a chair and slung it over her shoulder.

'Possibly,' said the Doctor and walked out onto the surface of the planet Kirith.

Not far from where the incongruous shape of a 1960s London police box had landed a young man sat in the shelter of a tree, watching the waves and the rain as they crashed against the rocks and turned the ground to mud. He munched thoughtfully on a wafer he had taken from the small parcel beside him.

He was tall and handsome, with the lean body of a swimmer, and his dark almond-shaped eyes sparkled in his finely chiselled face. As he pulled back his long wet hair he wished, not for the first time tonight, that he hadn't ventured out into the wilderness in this weather. Unfortunately he very seldom listened to his friends' advice.

But his sensible, level-headed, unimaginative friends did not have the dreams he had. They had begun a year ago as a nagging voice in his sleep, calling his name and whistling an indistinct but oddly familiar tune. He had gone to a physician who had provided him with a deltawave augmentor on the back of his neck which had given him dreamless sleep for some months. But the dreams fought back and when they finally returned they were stronger and more vivid than ever.

In his dreams his black hair was short and closely

21

cropped, so he knew he was fourteen again, his days his own while his teachers and the Brethren debated his future following his parents' death. He would spend his time in the highlands and the moors where the view of the stars was best, or on the cliffs or shore, looking out for hours at the vast and formless sea. Usually he was alone, but occasionally he was aware of someone else, a friendly laughing presence. But when he turned to look there was nothing but an indistinct blur beside him.

Then the last dream came. Though he could see nothing he knew that he was sitting somewhere by the seashore. It was a sunny day, the weather gloriously warm. With a branch he was glumly prodding the skull of a dead cat. The words in his head rang as clear and distinct as a bell.

'I think you're mad to go.'

'My mother thinks it's a good idea. And so does Revna.'

'What does Revna know? All she's interested in is herself. With you out of the way she can be Mummy's little girl again.'

'But it's a once-in-a-lifetime opportunity. I need to practise, study. My playing hasn't been as good as it used to be.'

'It sounds good enough to me. And ten years! With only that miserable bunch of geriatrics and their creepy servants for company.'

'You shouldn't talk disrespectfully of the Panjistri — or their companions!'

'Why not? They can't hear us up here. So when do you go?'

'A few months' time. I leave for Kandasi by the Harbours, after some instruction from Huldah —'

'And there's another boring old goat for you! Do you really want to spend the next ten years of your life with people like that?'

'Raphael, you're my best friend. Even if you don't

22

approve, be at the Harbours when I go.'

'Just don't expect me to look after your sister when you're gone. And I still think you're mad!'

The next day he had told Revna of the dream, but she had just looked at him blankly. She had never had a brother, she had told him frostily; if he didn't believe her he could always ask her mother.

Over the following days the dream returned to him, nagging at his brain even during the day, until he resolved somehow to seek out the place he had been in his dream.

So it was that he now found himself, sheltering under a tree on a storm-cracked night, trying to make sense of the teasing half-memories which buzzed infuriatingly around his mind. He sat there for hours, fruitless hours when he silently went over his suspicions. His dreams, he felt, were not imaginings but forgotten memories which needed only the right stimulus to be reawakened.

And then as he stared up at the twin moons of Kirith the vague memories and suspicions finally coalesced into a sudden and painful flash of remembrance.

Raphael became the first person in ten years to remember Darien, the musician who went to join the Panjistri on the island of Kandasi.

Like a blind man suddenly given sight, Raphael became confused and disorientated as the memories of his friend crashed indiscriminately into his mind with cruel vividness. He remembered the childhood games he and Darien played together, the teasing of Darien's older sister; he remembered the teenage scrapes they had got into, how Darien had taken the blame when it had really been Raphael who had scrawled the childish (but true) graffiti about Lord Huldah's personal habits on the Council House wall; he remembered his friend's music (but not the times when it had made him fall asleep); he remembered the Lord Reptu instructing Darien to say goodbye to all his

23

friends at the Harbours of the Chosen ten years ago.

Ten years ago!

Raphael stumbled to his feet. Tears of unfamiliar anger and despair filled his eyes and he looked wildly about, unsure where to turn. Finally, like everyone else on Kirith, he looked seawards.

There through the driving rain and hail, serene and admonishing in its fastness, was the island of Kandasi.

The sky cracked open as a sheet of lightning illuminated the night. Hidden behind a tree Raphael thought he could see a dark shape: he could make out a blue frightened face and eyes which gleamed in the sudden light, and then vanished. Startled, and disturbed by the noise and sudden brilliance, Raphael turned and lost his footing on the slippery rocks of the shore. With a cry he fell headlong into the water, gashing his side on the needle-sharp rocks.

The waves dragged him mercilessly along down the narrow channel which led to the open sea. Frantically he tried to gain control and swim against the current, making for the overhanging trees and branches along the shore. But his boots and bulky clothing hampered his movements and the flow of the water was too strong. Like a spider remorselessly drawing in a fly the current carried him further and further down the bay towards the mouth of the open sea.

A piece of driftwood smashed him in the face, and hot blood streamed down into his eyes. The world swam about him and his vision became blurred and dizzy. Salt water gushed into his mouth making him retch.

Then dimly he heard voices above the roar of the wind and the sea, and through his daze he thought he saw someone on the shore. It was a girl with one arm around an overhanging tree and the other around the waist of an older man, who was reaching out to him with a long stick.

Dreamily Raphael realized that they were trying to save

him and with numb, aching fingers he grabbed the curled end of the man's stick. Grunting with exertion and cursing in a long-dead language, the man dragged Raphael's almost unconscious body ashore.

Raphael heard the girl shout above the roar of the wind. 'Professor, is he —?'

The man in the brown coat and oddly patterned jumper shook his head. Raphael was aware of him checking both sides of his chest for his double heartbeat. 'He's bleeding badly; there might be concussion,' the man cried out. 'We must get him some medical treatment.'

'Back to the TARDIS then?'

'Definitely not. We must take him to the town.'

'How do we know where that is?'

'Follow me. I know the way.'

And then Raphael blacked out.

Chapter 3

Kirith town stood proudly atop a hill on a small peninsula, only fifteen minutes' walk from where the TARDIS had landed. But in the biting wind and hail the Doctor and Ace found the going treacherous. Raphael kept drifting in and out of consciousness, hindering the two travellers even further as they struggled to support his weight between them. Their feet slipped and then stuck in the mud, and wind-tossed brambles and bushes ripped at their clothing.

Concerned though she was with Raphael, Ace was also wondering what reception they would receive when they reached the town. In her admittedly limited experience, she had found most alien races to have an innate distrust of strangers coupled with an annoying wish to make her and the Doctor's life as uncomfortable as possible. As tactfully as she could in the circumstances, she pointed this out to the Doctor, who merely pooh-poohed the idea and asked her where her faith in human nature was.

'Don't worry, Ace,' he reassured her, 'this is Kirith. They'll welcome us with open arms, trust me. When have I ever lied to you?'

Plenty of times, thought Ace. And why are you so sure if you've never been here before? And while we're on the subject how do you know the way so well?'

A flash of lightning illuminated the sky and the Doctor pointed up to the top of the hill.

Forgetting for a moment the weather and her burden, Ace gasped in admiration. 'Professor ... it's beautiful.'

Silhouetted in the silvery-blue lightning flash, Kirith town perched high on the rocks, impassive to the storm which raged about it. As immovable and as permanent as the pyramids of Egypt or the stones on Salisbury Plain, it appeared to be an unfeeling sentinel coolly surveying the land about it. It seemed to grow out of the black rock as naturally as the tempest-tossed trees at its base.

A steep stone stairway, its steps worn down by the passage of time, led past outlying buildings to the first level of the town — a large courtyard, somewhat sheltered from the weather. There the Doctor and Ace paused to rest with their burden and take a better look at the town towering above them.

A further stairway climbed to rugged ramparts and a turreted barbican which surrounded the town proper. A set of ornate golden gates stood open as if in welcome and beyond them a winding cobbled road snaked its way up through innumerable small buildings of red and weathered stone. In each of them warm friendly lights shone through windows of stained and coloured glass. Arching over the road and its adjoining streets electric lights hummed and crackled softly.

As the road climbed further up so the buildings became grander. The red stone of the lower buildings was now replaced by white polished stone and green speckled marbled pillars. Slate roofs gave way to leaded roofs and domes of silver and gold.

And at the very summit, nestled among the towers and onion domes, stood the main building of the town, the Council House, a cathedral-like structure of austere and

27

reproving beauty. Seemingly built of elaborately carved pillars of darkest ebony, it dominated the town. Its tall Gothic spire, tipped with purest crystal, sparkled in the lightning. Ace was reminded of both the faraway majesty of the Kremlin and the medieval splendour of the Mont Saint-Michel in Normandy.

'Intriguing blend of architectural styles,' remarked the Doctor. 'I wonder what King Charles would have to say about it?'

'It's magnificent,' breathed Ace. By her side the young man groaned.

'We'd better get a move on,' said the Doctor. 'He's in need of urgent medical help, and look −' he pointed up to the open gates − 'we have a welcoming committee.'

'Come on then, sunshine,' she said resignedly and helped Raphael to his feet as the Doctor took his other arm. 'If we're going to get locked up in the castle dungeon it might as well be now.'

'Ace,' reproved the Doctor and started to climb the steps.

At the open gates to the town a group of men dressed in scarlet velvet tunics and high laced boots were waiting for them. Their leader was a tall man with fine greying hair, a hooked nose and sharp, piercing eyes set in hollowed sockets; he appeared to be about seventy years old. He made a signal, and four of his companions rushed forward and took the unconscious Raphael from the Doctor and Ace.

'Hey, where do you think you're taking him?'

'Please don't worry, young lady,' he said. 'Raphael will be cared for and you may see him tomorrow.'

'Hello, I'm the Doctor and this is my friend Ace,' offered the Doctor and doffed a very wet and bedraggled hat which, in spite of the wind, had somehow stayed firmly on his head.

28

The tall man smiled in welcome. 'And I am Miríl,' he said, accenting the second syllable. He held out a bony hand in welcome. 'Please accept my thanks for Raphael's safe return. He was warned about travelling abroad in this weather, but the youth of today ... well, what can you do?' He raised his eyes heavenwards and sighed.

'I know just what you mean,' grinned the Doctor and glanced at Ace. 'I have the same problem myself.'

Ace glared back at him.

Miríl looked them up and down. 'You are wet,' he remarked — just a little too drily, thought Ace. 'Perhaps you'd like to come up into the town? The least I can do is arrange quarters and shelter for you.'

'That would be splendid,' said the Doctor. 'Tell me, is the weather always like this?'

'Of course not, Doctor,' he replied, surprised at the question. 'Yesterday some of our youngsters were sunbathing on the shore. Tomorrow it may snow.'

'There you are, Ace, you should feel right at home,' said the Doctor. 'Just like England.'

They walked slowly up the spiralling path which led to the seminary where Miríl lived and he introduced himself as a teacher, one of the minor officials of Kirith. The hours were long and the rewards few, he complained bitterly, but he did have access to one of the finest libraries on the planet; perhaps the Doctor and Ace would like to spend some time with him there tomorrow?

'I'd rather see the sights,' chirped in Ace. 'You know, leaning towers, hanging gardens, that sort of thing.'

Miríl sighed, once again bemoaning the frivolity of the young.

'I, however, would be delighted to take a look at your library,' said the Doctor quickly, but not without a knowing wink at Ace. 'Fascinating things, libraries. Full of the dust of the past and the promise of the future. Tell me, Miríl, do you know anything about artron energy?'

'No.'

'I thought not . . . So here we are!'

They stood before the massive oaken doors of the seminary of Kirith, a breathtaking building carved out of granite. Intricate carvings and ledges adorned the walls, between which crept purple and green ivy; the arched windows were covered with stark iron railings. It was a building which looked as though it could withstand with ease siege and famine, flood and disaster. Carved over the door was a legend in some alien language.

To Ace's surprise the door was opened by a middle-aged woman dressed in a tunic similar to Miríl's; Ace kicked herself for supposing that all the teachers on this plane would be male.

Miríl introduced his colleague as Tanyel and she received them with the same studied politeness and equanimity shown them earlier.

'You must be in need of refreshment,' she said stiffly. 'Please, follow me.'

The Doctor stopped Ace from pulling a face behind her back as Tanyel and Miríl led the two travellers to a small refectory where a meal of meats and spiced wine was already waiting for them.

As they passed through the seminary they took in their surroundings. Elaborate and beautiful tapestries decorated the walls of the seminary's winding passageways; at one point they passed through an indoor courtyard where a fountain of crystal sparkled in the light of the moons, which shone down through a porphyry dome overhead.

In other places banks of computers lined the walls, tinkling and chattering to each other, and spewing out information to their operators. Seminarians were sitting at them, keying notes into desktop computers. It was a curious mix of baroque splendour and modern technology, noted the Doctor, and remarkable for the fact that both styles complemented each other to make a complete and pleasing whole.

'Technology need not preclude beauty, Doctor,' intoned Tanyel. Ace thought she sounded just like a museum guide, and her impression was confirmed when she was told not to touch any of the objects she saw around her.

As they walked, they were greeted by other teachers and seminarians, all of whom regarded the Doctor and Ace with undisguised curiosity, smiled and then went on their way. No matter their age, and some were almost as young as Ace, everyone they met was strikingly good looking.

The teachers, Tanyel elaborated, were administrators and educators, responsible for the general wellbeing of the people of Kirith. They ensured that each member of society had enough to eat and adequate opportunity to express himself or herself in whatever manner they chose. They were answerable only to the Lord Procurator Huldah and the Brethren, a small band of powerful men and women, linked by complicated ties of blood and ability, who ruled the towns dotted about the surface of the planet.

And then, of course, there were the Panjistri.

'Oh? And who are they?' The Doctor's interest was aroused.

Tanyel looked at the Doctor guardedly, and then glanced back at Miríl as though looking for advice.

'The Panjistri are the ultimate providers,' he explained. 'They are our benefactors and our guardians. Everything you see here is in the gift of the Panjistri: they reveal to us the mysteries of science and ensure that our food supplies never diminish. They are the source of all our comforts, so that we may live our lives fully for the benefit of all.'

31

'Just like having a nanny,' the Doctor said under his breath, and then: 'I'd very much like to meet one of these Panjistri.'

'That, of course, will be impossible, Doctor,' Tanyel said, standing aside as she opened a door. She gave him a frosty smile and turned to leave. Reminding the Doctor that he would be delighted to show him the library in the morning, Miríl followed her.

'This place makes me uncomfortable, Professor,' said Ace when Miríl and Tanyel had left.

'Whatever for?' asked the Doctor, helping himself to a glass of hot spiced wine.

Ace threw her wet jacket and rucksack on to a sumptuous chaise longue. 'There's something not right about the whole set-up. Everyone's too nice. No one wants to know who we are or what we're doing here.'

'Why should they? We don't mean any harm.'

'But if two total strangers came up to me, with a half-dead body in tow, I'd at least think there was something dodgy going on. What's up? Why's everyone accepting us?'

'Perhaps they've been expecting us,' the Doctor said mysteriously. 'Or perhaps the Kirithons are just the most trusting race in the universe?'

'So why do I feel that I'm going to be murdered in my bed tonight?'

'A little trust, Ace, that's all it takes.'

I trusted people on Earth and on Iceworld, she thought, and they all used me. My friend Manisha nearly died from trusting that no bastard was going to try to burn her house down. The only person I trust now is you, Professor; so why do I feel there's something you're not telling me?

But Ace kept those thoughts to herself.

Tanyel looked aghast.

'The strangers are obviously not of our world, and in such an instance the instructions are quite explicit,' she repeated in her clipped tone. 'They must be accorded all due civility and comforts, and the Brethren must be immediately informed.'

'And so, they shall,' said Miríl. 'But not immediately. Let me talk with the man first of all. He has great knowledge; he has much that I could learn.'

'What can he know that we cannot access in the libraries?'

Miríl looked heavenwards and his eyes sparkled greedily. 'What lies beyond our world, Tanyel. We don't have the technology to travel to the stars, but the Doctor has. Haven't you ever wondered what is out there, Tanyel?'

Tanyel sniffed haughtily, and smoothed back her finely coiffed white hair. 'All that lies beyond is but bleakness and despair.' She intoned the litany she had learnt at school. 'The Matriarch provides and I am contented . . . Nothing else matters.'

'We had space travellers here once before, almost two hundred years ago, so the records tell me,' said Miríl. 'But the Rills joined the Brotherhood of Kandasi before we learnt anything from them.'

'Then I envy them that honour. I would give my life to become a true acolyte of the Panjistri,' retorted Tanyel. 'But the presence of the outsiders here disturbs the balance and order of our society. Would you have Kirith descend into chaos and want? The Brethren must be told.'

'The Brethren already know,' came a deep and ponderous voice.

Miríl and Tanyel turned to see the figure which had been listening behind a pillar.

'L-lord Huldah,' stammered Tanyel, and curtsied as his huge bulk moved out of the shadows, 'I wasn't aware . . .'

33

'The Brethren are everywhere, Tanyel,' said Huldah. He turned to Miríl, who acknowledged him with a reluctant nod and greeted him through clenched teeth.

'Miríl, the Brethren ask very little and offer you everything. Don't let your thirst for knowledge interfere with your responsibilities to us and the Panjistri.' There was no mistaking the implied threat in Huldah's voice.

'The coming of the two strangers has already been noted,' he continued. 'Grant them every comfort — for the time being.'

Ace awoke the following morning in a sumptuous four-poster bed with the sun streaming in through the beaded windows of her bedroom. She was pleasantly surprised to discover that her throat had not been cut during the night. Maybe the Doctor was right after all, and she should start trusting people a little more.

A silk dressing gown had been left for her and as she put it on she idly wondered how much one of the rich trendies in the Portobello Road would pay for it. Her clothes from last night had all been washed and dried and were carefully folded at the foot of the bed.

There was a wonderful smell and she saw at the far end of the room a small metal table already laden with hot breads, and fruits, cheeses and honey. Some room service, she thought as she munched on the most delicious apple she had tasted in her life; it sure beats the cholesterol gunk at Mrs Smith's boarding house in East London.

Looking out of the window she saw no evidence of last night's storm. Instead the sun was shining on what seemed to be a gloriously hot day, and the winding streets of the town were already packed with Kirithons taking their early morning stroll. Doesn't anyone work here, she asked herself. A knock at the door interrupted her thoughts.

'Come in,' she said and then started with surprise as

34

she saw who it was.

'Hello, I'm Raphael,' the newcomer said brightly. 'You must be Ace. I believe you saved my life.'

Ace had last seen Raphael bleeding and unconscious and very close to death. Now his face glowed and there was no trace of the cruel wound on his forehead or the bruising around his eyes. He walked into the room with the lithe agility of a dancer, his appearance totally belying the fact that only hours earlier his side had been gashed open by the jagged rocks. If Ace didn't know better she would have said that he had just returned from a few weeks' holiday at a particularly luxurious health farm.

She also noticed just how attractive Raphael was.

'You're . . . you're better,' she blurted out.

Raphael smiled. With those gorgeous white teeth, Ace thought. 'Yes. I'd have come earlier but Miríl spent the whole of breakfast giving me a lecture.'

'But you were half dead. How did you recover so quickly?'

Raphael looked at her curiously. 'Oh, my side, you mean. That was what Miríl was complaining about: he had to spend most of the night fixing it up. Kept him away from his boring old books, he said.' Without any self-consciousness Raphael lifted up his shirt. The skin was smooth and tanned − there was no trace of any wound or scar. Ace couldn't understand.

'Don't you have retroactive surgery in your town?' he asked her, and before she could answer, 'Where do you come from anyway?'

'Perivale,' Ace answered without thinking.

'Peri-vale. Is that past the Darkfell?' Raphael was intrigued.

'Yes, that's right,' Ace replied, thinking that the new name sounded like a second-rate heavy metal band.

'Would you take me sometime?' he asked as eagerly

35

as a little boy asking for a trip to the circus. 'The Brethren don't like us going anywhere near there; they say it's too dangerous and the land is poisonous.'

'Oh, it's not quite that bad yet,' she replied, wondering what she was letting herself in for.

Before Raphael could pursue the subject there was an exaggerated cough behind them. Ace turned to see a stunningly beautiful woman standing in the doorway. Her flame-coloured hair was short and impeccably styled, and though her mouth was warm and tender, there was a particular hardness in her eyes.

The woman looked Ace up and down with obvious distaste, and Ace instantly felt inferior. This woman reminded her uncomfortably of her schooldays as a spotty kid, jealous of the exploits of the older, more attractive and assured girls. Disregarding Ace, the woman addressed Raphael.

'There you are,' she said. Her tone was frosty, but when she looked at Raphael some tenderness apeared in her steely eyes. 'Lord Huldah wants to see you in the Council House immediately.'

Raphael groaned. 'What for?'

'I imagine to reprimand you for your little excursion last night. You should really do as you're told, Raphael. It's for everyone's benefit, after all. Whatever were you doing out at night anyway?'

Raphael frowned and suddenly looked troubled. For some strange reason he found it difficult to remember.

'All right, Revna, I'm coming,' he said and made for the door. He looked back at Ace. 'Shall I see you later?'

Ace shrugged. ''Spose so. If you want to.'

'Come on, Raphael!' Revna shot a glint of pure venom at Ace. Raphael grinned helplessly at her and then followed Revna.

Ace turned sulkily back to her breakfast table and

36

chewed violently on a piece of bread. Just because I'm talking to her boyfriend she treats me like dirt, she thought angrily. Well, as far as I'm concerned Glamour Puss can keep him.

'Having fun making enemies, Ace?'

'Professor! How long have you been there?'

'Long enough,' the Doctor said meaningfully and walked in through the open door. 'So what did you think of our orphan of the storm?'

'Raphael? It's well weird, Professor. Last night he was almost dead, right? Now he's up and about like nothing happened. He said something about retroactive surgery.'

'A highly advanced technique,' the Doctor explained and noticed a red patch on Ace's arm. 'Hurt yourself?'

'Must have scratched myself in the night; it's nothing.'

The Doctor nodded, and continued: 'Surgery wouldn't account for the lack of scars, however ...' He rubbed his chin thoughtfully. 'Acute tissue regeneration? I've seen that before on Alzarius; it's part of a rapid adaptation to changing environmental circumstances.'

'Like the weather,' Ace added helpfully.

The Doctor shaded his eyes and looked out of the window into the sunny streets. 'Yes, these freak weather conditions are apparently normal on this planet. Strange that. A hiccough in Paradise.'

'What do you mean, Professor?'

'Take a look around you, Ace. Everything's so perfect.' He pulled back a tapestry and ran his hand over the smooth surface of the plaster wall. 'No cracks.'

He pushed open the window and indicated the people in the street. 'Look at them, all smiling, all happy, all perfectly content with their lot.'

Ace looked at the faces down below. 'And there's another thing, Professor,' she said. 'They're all so good looking; there's not a naff one among them. But ...'

'Yes?' The Doctor encouraged her: it was taking time but she was getting there.

'Well, it's a weird, blank sort of beauty. Like a third-rate Aussie soap star.' A sudden idea struck her. 'I've got it! They're robots, right? Androids?'

The Doctor shook his head. 'Androids don't bleed, or grow old.' He walked over to the table and smeared a chunk of bread with some honey. 'I don't like perfection, Ace. It dulls the spirit, numbs the mind. If everything's perfect then there's no need to progress. Everyone needs the right to be unhappy with their lot from time to time.' He winked at her. 'I have to see Miríl; why don't you go after Raphael and have him show you the sights? I think it's time to cause a few more hiccoughs in Paradise, don't you?'

Ace grinned. 'You bet, Professor!'

Chapter 4

The Lord Procurator Huldah knows best — it was a universally accepted truth in this small town, one of many on Kirith. Scion of a noble family before such distinctions had been abolished, he had set his cousins and relatives in positions of power among the Brethren, and he ruled them all with a benevolent if at times ruthless hand. Loyal to no one except himself and the Panjistri, he knew what the people of Kirith wanted and calmly but resolutely went out and got it for them.

Some said it was his childhood that had made him so strong-minded and superior. Once, when Miríl's tongue had been loosened by too much wine, he had revealed how Huldah had been bullied constantly as a boy. With a determination almost shocking in a child he had exercised and built his muscles until no one dared bully him again. Nor did he neglect his mind; he would spend late nights reading all the records in the library, to the exclusion of social contact with others his own age. Under the influence of the wine, Miríl revealed that he suspected Huldah knew even more than he.

Huldah's devotions had attracted the attention of the Panjistri themselves, and Huldah asked that he be considered for acceptance into the Brotherhood of Kandasi. They refused, explaining that he would better serve them as their ambassador, guiding the Kirithons in their every-day life and ensuring that their wishes were carried out to the full.

Over the years, Huldah had grown fat with power, but there was still a dark and strong handsomeness about his face, though his skin was now sallow and his beard streaked with grey. He still ruled Kirith with his own brand of fairness: everyone had all they could wish for and some, particularly if they were young and especially attractive, had more.

All these thoughts were going through Raphael's mind as he waited outside Huldah's apartments where Revna, proud of her position as Huldah's personal assistant, had left him like a naughty schoolboy summoned before the headmaster.

Raphael reflected on the inquisition and inevitable lecture to come. This wouldn't be the first time he had been called up in front of Huldah, he thought glumly; there had been the incident with the stink bomb when he was a child and later the time when he had spied on Huldah and two of his 'special' friends. But life could be so dull at times: Kirith needed a little bit of excitement every now and then.

The door to Huldah's personal office opened and Raphael was called inside.

Huldah was seated at his desk — a finely polished piece of mahogany — and was engrossed in paperwork. As Raphael entered, his feet sank into the plush carpet. Huldah looked up briefly and the glow from the computer screens at his side bathed his face in a ghastly green light. He indicated for Raphael to sit down in front of the desk and continued with his work.

Refusing to be upset by this studied indifference, Raphael occupied himself by looking around the room. The wall behind Huldah was a huge bookcase, filled with ancient volumes, papers and computer disks. Paintings covered another wall, together with studies, some tasteful, some much less so of the female form. A third wall was occupied by a series of video screens showing various parts of the town: of the views, he recognized, among others, the great library, the small bay to the east where the Panjistri disembarked from their home, the sea cliffs looking out to Kandasi, and the forbidden Darkfell. Most of the fourth wall was taken up by a marble fireplace in which burned a massive wood fire which scented the room with a sickly-sweet fragrance, making him feel light-headed. It was a curious mixture of styles; if he had learnt the right vocabulary from Ace, Raphael would have called it well gross and tacky.

He became aware that the scratching of pen on paper had stopped. Huldah looked up at the boy with the affectionate eyes and welcoming smile of the crocodile at the first sight of Captain Hook.

'Yes, I do like my comforts, Raphael,' said Huldah and put his papers away to one side. 'A real log fire is so much more friendly, don't you think?' He clasped his hands and leaned forward to look into Raphael's eyes; the boy caught the distinct smell of alcohol on his breath.

'You have caused us a great deal of trouble and concern, Raphael,' he said. His voice was critical, but not unkind. 'This is not the first of your secret midnight excursions. All on Kirith are free and we do not set rules. But we do expect cooperation; and we ask — only ask — that no one goes outside the boundaries of the town at night without our permission.'

'But why?'

'There are dangers in the forest and fells. A man may stray and lose his way. The wilds of Darkfell run foul with poisons.' Huldah spoke as though to a little child. 'Why did you leave the town, Raphael? Everything is provided

41

for you here, isn't it?'

Huldah's kind manner disconcerted Raphael. 'Of course, Lord Huldah, and I'm grateful. But the stars are much more beautiful outside. I just wanted to be alone.'

'In the middle of a storm?'

Raphael frowned. Now that he mentioned it it did seem a lame excuse. What had possessed him to go out on such a night? 'Well, I wasn't the only one,' he blurted out in his defence.

Huldah's eyes narrowed, searching into Raphael's own. 'There was Ace, and the Doctor,' he said quickly, judging it wiser not to mention the other figure he had seen on the shore.

Huldah leaned forward and grabbed Raphael by the wrist. He winced at the older man's powerful grip. 'You are not to associate with the Doctor and his companion, do you understand?' The kindly manner was gone. 'They are disruptive elements, alien to our work here on Kirith.'

'And there was Darien!' Raphael blurted out as the memory suddenly returned to him. 'What happened to Darien? Why did I forget him?'

For long seconds Huldah said nothing and continued to stare at Raphael. His nails digging deep into the flesh, he increased his grip on the boy's arm. When he finally spoke Raphael was surprised to notice a slight tremor in Huldah's threatening tone.

'Darien has accepted the greatest honour of all and become an acolyte of the Panjistri. He is not to be spoken of again. Do so and you die.'

For the first time in his life Raphael was afraid. 'Of . . . of course, Lord Procurator,' he stammered.

Huldah relaxed his grip, leant back in his chair and smiled. 'Good. We may not always understand the ways of the Panjistri but all their decisions are for our ultimate benefit. Now, if we understand each other, you may go.'

As soon as Raphael left Huldah broke out in a cold sweat. He hurried over to the bank of video screens on the wall facing him. As he approached, one of the screens lit up instantly, revealing the face of a stern old man.

'Your report, Huldah,' demanded Reptu.

The change in Huldah's manner was remarkable. Normally self-assured, he stumbled over his words whenever he faced a member of the Panjistri, even at a distance over a video link.

'Raphael has broken through your conditioning, my lord,' he said in a tone which suggested that he held himself wholly responsible for the fact. 'He is beginning to remember. What should I do?'

Expecting at the very least an angry outburst, he waited for Reptu's reply. Instead, Reptu paused for a moment, considering the matter. When he addressed Huldah again there was a slight smile on his face.

'The boy shows great imagination and courage,' he said. 'He may be of use to us. For the moment let him walk free, but take care that he keeps his memories to himself.'

The image faded from the screen. Huldah let out a sigh of relief. Loyal as he was to the Panjistri, they were nevertheless an unpleasant reminder that he was not the absolute ruler of Kirith town. Yet without them he would be nothing. The deal he had struck with them was advantageous enough: assured power over all his subjects in return for his recruiting the best and most talented Kirithons into their service. If only the Panjistri weren't so obviously superior: they had even known about the arrival of the Doctor and Ace before Huldah's spies.

Sometimes Huldah wondered why the Panjistri were so eager for new entrants into the Brotherhood of Kandasi. But he valued his position too much to ask such dangerous questions.

***

43

Ace, on the other hand, was doing nothing but asking questions. For once she was following the Doctor's advice, and was looking for Raphael. Already something of a minor celebrity in the small town, she found most people eager to talk to her and ready to offer any help they could.

Finally she was told that Raphael was at the Council House in the presence of the Lord Procurator Huldah. There was no need for security in Kirith and Ace wandered into the spectacular building without anyone attempting to stop her.

As she turned a corner she walked straight into Huldah himself, causing him to drop the sheaf of files he was carrying.

'I'm sorry,' she said as she bent down to help him pick up his papers, 'I wasn't looking where I was going.'

Huldah dismissed the incident with a wave of a finely manicured hand. 'No need to worry, my dear, no harm done,' he said, offering her his sweetest smile. He looked her up and down with interest, and Ace felt uncomfortable under his gaze. 'It's rare that we have such a pretty young thing about the place.'

He's making fun of me, was her first thought. Compared to the rest of the women in this town I might as well look like the back end of a bus. She looked behind her, just to make sure he wasn't talking to someone else. 'Do you mean me?' She grinned in embarrassment and jumped as he took hold of her arm.

'Don't be frightened, my dear,' he continued confidently, a lascivious leer on his face. 'Might I suggest that we go elsewhere to continue our conversation? You are such a pretty young thing, after all.'

Ace wrested her arm from his grasp, her indignation rising to the surface.

'Now look here, scum-features,' she hissed through clenched teeth. 'You lay another finger on me and I'll make

sure you won't be able to do anything with any "pretty
young things" ever again. Get the picture?' She raised a
tightly clenched fist to make her point.

Huldah stepped back less in fear than in amazement:
no one had ever refused the advances of the Lord
Procurator before. Then he smiled almost triumphantly,
and rubbed his hands in glee. Such fiery spirit! Such
aggression! Here was prize sport indeed!

Ace turned gratefully as she heard the sound of
approaching footsteps. It was the unpleasant young woman
she had seen earlier this morning. Revna stopped and
looked first at Huldah, and then at Ace, swiftly assessing
the situation. Then she turned back to Huldah, nodding
him a greeting.

'My Lord, your presence is requested by the Lord Reptu
again,' she announced primly.

Huldah continued to stare at Ace as he replied: 'I have
much to tell them.' As he left he bowed in mock courtesy
to Ace and winked suggestively at her. 'I'll see you later,
my dear.'

Not if I see you first, bilge-brain, Ace thought, and as
soon as he had turned the corner she asked Revna, 'Who's
the prize creep then?'

'The Lord Procurator Huldah,' she said coldly and then
hissed: 'What do you think you're doing here? Can't you
mind your own business?'

'Hey, if that's all that's bothering you, Huldah's all
yours!' she said lightly, attempting to defuse the situation.
The moment she had spoken she realized she had said the
wrong thing.

'You know exactly what I mean,' Revna continued in
a harsh whisper. 'You're doing Raphael no good, filling
his head with new ideas. You'll only make him restless
and put him in more danger.'

I don't believe it, she's acting like a jealous schoolgirl!

45

'Look, it might have escaped your notice but me and the Professor saved your boyfriend from drowning last night —'

'He's not my boyfriend —'

'And as for fancying him you've got it all wrong. He's not my type — he's too pretty for one thing. You can keep him — and Huldah as well if you like,' she added viciously and stormed off in anger.

'Where are you going?'

'To find Raphael,' she called back and found to her delight that she didn't care what Revna thought at all.

Two huge battle cruisers stealthily approached the tiny brown planet hanging defenceless and alone in the blackness of space. Beeping messages passed between the two engines of death as they each coordinated their strategies, assessing the best positions from which to attack.

Suddenly from the far side of the planet a posse of small red flying creatures appeared, their wings waving and flapping furiously in the airless zero gravity. Splitting into two formations they clustered around each of the two spaceships, which panicked and attempted to retreat. Chattering excitedly to each other in the soundless void the flying creatures closed in on the trapped craft, eating through their force-field defences and into their metal hulls.

The Universe exploded in a flash of brilliant light as the creatures devoured their prey.

Beaming with satisfaction and self-congratulation the Doctor took his hand off the joystick of the desktop computer and grinned. 'My game again, Miríl?'

The older man's face was set firm, still entranced by the game he had just lost to the Doctor. One of his colleagues walked past them, looking disapprovingly at Miríl, and he instantly remembered where he was.

'A ... a fascinating application of the computer, Doctor, but hardly the use for which it was made,' he protested.

The Doctor patted him on the back like a long-lost friend. 'Quite right,' he said. 'But what's life without a little *divertissement* from time to time, eh?'

'The Panjistri would not approve.'

'I'm quite sure they wouldn't. But sometimes it's fun breaking the rules,' said the Doctor, deliberately leading the old man on. 'You could easily program the computer like I did — couldn't you?'

Miríl shook his head. 'The computer performs the purpose it was made for — to teach and to provide information. Nothing else.'

So you can operate the computer but you can't program it, thought the Doctor. He let the matter drop and then said casually: 'The Panjistri ... I'd like to hear more about them. Anyone who could provide all of this must be a very advanced and cultured people indeed.'

He looked around him at his surroundings. Early this morning Miríl had eagerly escorted him to his seminary's library, the largest of its kind on Kirith. It was housed in a splendid series of rooms, almost ecclesiastical in their restrained magnificence. At intervals along the walls magnificent stained glass windows, depicting mythical creatures, let in the sunlight.

The bulk of the library's collection was stored in a huge circular chamber, the size of a small cathedral and built on several levels. Teachers, in their formal dress of scarlet tunic and boots, sat at long banks of desks, studying ancient manuscripts or digesting the information relayed to them by desktop computers. Hidden lighting suffused the entire room with a warm and soothing glow, and the air buzzed with the soft murmur of study.

Further reading rooms and libraries led from the main

library like the spokes of a wheel; the corridors linking them were decorated with beautifully crafted sculptures, fine paintings, and restrained and tasteful experiments in abstract art. The Doctor had been in many libraries — he had lent his reader's ticket for the British Museum to Marx, advised Pope Clement on the contents of the Vatican Library, and even saved two plays by Aristophanes from the burning of the library in Alexandria — but the beautiful surroundings, the wealth of knowledge available and the diligence of those partaking of it impressed even him.

'The Panjistri are indeed an advanced race, Doctor,' answered Miríl with a respect he did not accord the Brethren, the Doctor noted. 'They are our providers and our teachers, our benefactors and our ideal. They provide us with the food we eat, with the technology and comforts we need to live our lives to their greatest fulfilment.'

'Yes, I know all that, Miríl. But who are they? Where do they come from?'

Miríl led the Doctor out of the main library and into a smaller reading room where they disturbed a young seminarian reading a handsomely bound volume. On seeing the Doctor and Miríl he stood up nervously and left the room.

'Officially he shouldn't be here at all,' explained Miríl. 'This room is reserved for the senior teachers such as myself. I should report him to the Brethren.'

'But I see you do bend the rules occasionally, Miríl,' the Doctor observed wryly.

'No one should be hindered in the pursuit of knowledge,' he replied flatly, but a common bond had been forged between the two men.

Miríl pulled out the drawer of a filing cabinet and took out a laser disc which he inserted into a small video screen on the far wall. The screen lit up, revealing a series of stylized moving images: a sleek streamlined spaceship

48

landing on a deserted plain, a band of tall, aristocratic people disembarking.

'Three thousand eight hundred and thirty-three years ago, the Panjistri came to our world,' intoned Miríl, awkwardly reciting the words he and all Kirithons had first learnt in the schoolroom. 'With them they brought all the learning of their home planet, which had been destroyed in solar flares. At that time the people of Kirith were a backward race, primitive in their learning, forever scavenging the forests for food.'

The scene on the screen changed to one of a group of swarthy, dark-eyed and emaciated people, armed only with clubs and knives. Their lumbering gait, protruding jaw lines and broad foreheads reminded the Doctor of the early hominids he had encountered on the plains of Africa over a million years before the dawn of human civilization.

These creatures were confronting a large but bewildered beast, obviously the intended meal of the day. The Doctor winced as the creature was brutally cudgelled to the ground. All death disturbed him even if, like this, it was part of the natural order of things.

'The Panjistri banished the stalking beasts to the furthermost reaches of our planet. As we could no longer feed on the meat of the beast they provided us with *zavát* —'

The Doctor showed interest and Miríl explained. '*Zavát* is our main food source which, together with the fruits and seeds which fall from the trees, provides us with all the sustenance we need.'

The Doctor felt a certain grudging respect for the Panjistri as he considered the consequences of that simple action. The first need of any species is to find enough food to eat; from that basic requirement comes inevitably the skill of hunting, and from that comes the crafting of weapons, first of defence and survival and then of war

49

and aggression.

The bomb that fell on Hiroshima was but the direct descendant of the bone the first caveman had used to kill his prey. By freeing Kirith from the tyranny of hunger the Panjistri had effectively abolished war and helped the planet leapfrog many thousands of years of painful evolution. It was no small achievement.

'So the Panjistri care for all your needs, teach you their technology and its application,' summarized the Doctor, eager to be spared any more of Miríl's home movies. 'But what do they get in return?'

The picture on the screen was replaced by one of Kandasi Island. 'The Panjistri ask only for solitude on Kandasi, where they pursue their studies in peace. Occasionally some of our more gifted citizens elect to become members of their Brotherhood, helping them in their work.'

'Which is?'

Miríl smiled. 'That is their business, Doctor.'

Them that ask no questions don't get told no lies, thought the Doctor, but said instead: 'That sounds a very good deal indeed.'

'Of course, and we're all grateful for the munificence of the Panjistri, but ...' Miríl approached his subject warily.

'Yes?'

'There is much we can learn from your knowledge and experience,' said Miríl. 'You come from beyond our world, Doctor, from out among the stars. It is a place we can never go to; we are trapped on our planet.'

'Surely with all this technology you can ...'

Miríl shook his head. 'Not even the Panjistri can leave: no craft can escape the gravitational pull of our world.' Miríl looked greedily at the Doctor; and there was a peculiar disconcerting light in his eyes. 'Like the star travellers before you, Doctor, you must soon join the

Panjistri. But before then share your knowledge with me. Tell me of the other worlds you have seen, the secrets hidden in the star clusters. Tell me of the power of time . . .'

The Doctor froze, suddenly disconcerted by Miríl's change from wry academic to obsessive seeker of knowledge. He gave him a curious gaze, and then paced slowly around the room.

A minute passed. The Doctor took a coin from his pocket and casually flipped it into the air.

'I can tell you many things, Miríl,' he said. 'I can tell you of worlds beyond wonder and of a secret older than time. I can tell you of the nature of good and evil, the power of the human heart, and the best recipe for bread and butter pudding.'

He flicked the coin into the air once again, and the light from the video screen cast dark shadows about his face.

'But I'll tell you only two things. Those records you've shown me are a sham: there's not a word of truth in any of them. And you, the Panjistri and everyone else for that matter, could leave this planet whenever you want.

'You've been tricked, duped, Miríl. All your people have. The Panjistri need you much more than you need them. And I intend to find out why.'

Chapter 5

Where am I in this warmth and this dissonance? What are these feelings which flow around me and feed me, giving me power and adding to my knowledge?

When did I begin and what was there before me? Was Nothingness there before me? If there was Nothingness when did it become Some Thing?

Who is this alien presence I am aware of, and why am I so aware of him/her/it?

Why do these energies crackle and spark around me? What is their purpose?

What is my *purpose?*

Why?

So many questions, and no answers ... Yet.

As she had done for more than three thousand years, the Grand Matriarch, leader of the Panjistri and Provider for All Kirith, sat in her chambers on Kandasi, silently reflecting on the past and on the great task that had been entrusted her. Absent-mindedly she stroked the fur of the ever-faithful Fetch, who knelt by her side.

The day she and eighty-four of her colleagues had left her home world on the first part of their great mission was now a distant if still treasured memory.

Further back, she could remember taking the veil, renouncing all worldly pleasures and relations, and becoming a sister of the Panjistri. Four centuries later she could still smell the incense from the gold censers at the beginning of her novitiate, and hear her new brothers and sisters chanting in the Chapel of Renouncement, and the words of the Patriarch as he introduced her to the sacred mysteries. The memories of her initiation into the even deeper mysteries of her order and her eventual election a hundred years later to succeed the Patriarch as only the second Matriarch of the Panjistri still filled her with a rare and unaccustomed pride.

The Grand Matriarch's whole life was devoted to Kandasi. When other memories intruded upon her mind — the memory of the people and the lover she had left behind, the final vision of her planet as it was consumed by the solar flares — she chose to ignore and suppress them. Indeed, looking into the night sky she could not remember the exact location of her own star system.

Such memories were of no concern to the Panjistri. All that mattered was their great task. Nothing else was important.

Before her myriad screens shimmered in the darkness like the facets of a splendid jewel, each one feeding the Grand Matriarch with information from every part of Kirith. Not a leaf could fall, not a wind could blow, without the Grand Matriarch knowing about it.

Suddenly she stiffened and pointed a long bony finger at one particular screen. Alerted by his mistress's change of mood, Fetch leapt to his feet, his eyes darting around looking for danger. Reassured that all was in order, he looked at her quizzically.

The Grand Matriarch was pointing to a central screen on which was displayed a picture of the Doctor in discussion with Miríl.

'It is he,' she whispered, the excitement replacing her normal air of calm and cool detachment. 'We have all waited for this day for centuries. Our predictions said that one day he was bound to come here.'

'Mistress?' questioned Fetch. 'He's just a space traveller, one of many. He can be of use to us like all the others, but —'

'Not just a space traveller,' said the Matriarch, and her eyes blazed with green fire. 'This man calls himself the Doctor, and he always appears in times of greatest darkness. He brings with him a companion from a long-dead world.'

Another screen lit up and showed a picture of Ace. The Grand Matriarch clapped her hands with glee.

'At last, at last,' she crooned gently to herself. 'The missing pieces are now all in place and the game can begin.'

'Mistress?'

'Beware these two, Fetch,' she said, her tone changing abruptly once more. She indicated the two screens. 'Between them they possess a great and secret power. They have it in themselves to be our downfall — or our salvation.'

She paused and a thrill of sensual expectation ran through her tired and aching body. For the first time in many years she felt like a girl in the rosy flush of youth again. When she turned back to Fetch her face was beaming and her eyes were misty with joy.

'Tell the Panjistri to rejoice. Tell them that our moment of becoming is at hand. Our mission is drawing to its glorious close: at last the Omega Point is within sight!'

All save two video screens became dark; only the screens carrying the pictures of the Doctor and Ace remained bright. Then slowly the image of the Doctor faded from its screen.

The only face left was Ace's.

54

Chapter 6

Well, it certainly wasn't his fault, the scruffy little man thought miserably as he closed the TARDIS doors. It wasn't his fault that Polly had inexplicably taken it into her mind to leave the ship and wander off on her own; it wasn't his fault that she had got herself hopelessly lost in a strange alien town, and been reduced to tears; and it wasn't his fault that he hadn't stopped her going out in the first place.

So Polly had gone off in a huff to her room, and Ben had followed to calm her down. The little man looked about the empty control room, and reflected on the events of the past few weeks.

Ever since he had regenerated there had been a noticeable atmosphere of tension on board the TARDIS; even in the old days things had been much more relaxed. But now Ben, for instance, was suspicious of him, still not quite believing that he was who he said he was.

The scruffy little man allowed a flicker of self-doubt to enter his mind. Regeneration was a tricky business even for the most experienced Time Lord, and this regeneration had been his first. Perhaps the tension on board the ship was his fault; perhaps his regeneration wasn't working out quite as it should?

He dismissed the idea as preposterous and prepared the TARDIS for take-off. As the central column on the control console began to rise and fall and the familiar sound of dematerialization filled the room, the little man paused.

A shadow of suspicion darkened his brow. He felt somehow incomplete, as though he had left something behind somewhere. He patted his pockets, and grunted, satisfied that all their usual contents were still in place.

He gave a self-deprecating snort. It was nothing to worry about, probably only the after-effects of regeneration. And if he'd lost some of the infuriating arrogance of his first incarnation then that was all well and good.

Happy now, the little man began to tootle a merry tune on his recorder.

'What you are saying is heresy, Doctor,' protested Miríl. 'To even suggest that the Panjistri are deceiving us —'

' — Is nothing but the truth,' the Doctor interrupted passionately. 'You're a man of science and curiosity, Professor Travers —'

'Who?'

The Doctor raised a hand to his temple. 'Nonono, not Travers, I met him a long time ago . . .' He shook his head worriedly and rubbed his eyes.

'You're a man of great knowledge, Miríl,' he continued, 'but you'll never learn anything if you go around with your eyes closed.'

'What do you mean?'

The Doctor tapped out the code he had memorized when Miríl had activated the video screens. The familiar images reappeared on the screens.

'These home movies of the Panjistri, for one thing. How were they recorded?'

'The Panjistri were once a race of great telepaths,'

explained Miríl smugly. 'Even today some of them still retain that ability. They re-created these scenes from the memories stored in their minds.'

'How very clever of them,' retorted the Doctor. 'How very clever of them to remember a spacecraft whose structure couldn't even get them to the other side of this planet let alone halfway across the universe. A spacecraft that crossed a thousand parsecs of space without a single dent or buckle to its hull!'

Miríl frowned but he remained silent.

'And your so-called ancestors,' continued the Doctor relentlessly. 'Look at yourself in the mirror — you Kirithons are the most physically perfect people I've ever come across. You're tall, strong and athletic; see the difference in your ancestors!'

'I am not a child, Doctor,' reproved the older man. 'I do know of the process of evolution.'

The Doctor waved aside his protest. 'If they're your ancestors, then I congratulate you and your species, Miríl: your people have achieved in three thousand years what it took *homo sapiens* on Earth two million years to accomplish. Even with your amazing recuperative powers, evolution on such a time scale is simply impossible!'

Despite his outrage, Miríl's curiosity was beginning to get the better of him. 'What are you trying to say, Doctor?'

The Doctor threw up his hands in frustration. 'I don't know — yet. But the Panjistri are manipulating you for some reason.'

'How?'

'They've set you up in a comfortable little nest, provided you with everything you might want. Everything is done for you; you don't even have to look for food for yourselves. All you have to do is get on with your lives, idling away the time, taking whatever's offered you.'

'We have the technology to progress, Doctor —'

57

'But not the pioneering spirit!' cried the Doctor, his face now red with rage and frustration. 'I wonder how your species ever dragged itself out of the primeval slime. You have all the imagination of a stone!

'You're being spoonfed like babies. I doubt you could even grow potatoes without the Panjistri's help and permission. You never question the Panjistri's motives, or make any attempt to look beyond your own tiny little world. Oh no, if you did that it would upset your cosy little existence, wouldn't it? You're ... you're ...' He searched for the right word, and finally borrowed one from Ace's rich vocabulary. 'You're *wimps*!'

Miríl was taken aback, but the Doctor, now in full flow, hadn't finished yet. He took another coin out of his pocket and flicked it into the air, counting the seconds it took to fall to the ground. He made a series of rapid calculations to determine the strength of Kirith's gravity.

'The escape velocity on this planet is a little under six and a half miles per second; with the technology you possess you and the Panjistri could easily build spacecraft capable of leaving this planet. So why do the Panjistri want you to stay here?'

Miríl's face was white; his lips trembled and yet no sound came from them. The silence in the library was almost tangible. The Doctor had voiced suspicions that he had scarcely dared contemplate. 'You say we can reach the stars ...'

The Doctor nodded. 'If you applied the technology and science you have, yes.'

'Despite what you say, Doctor, like Raphael I have always wondered what lay beyond our world. I have always longed to see the marvels that I have only dreamt of. And yet you say that the Panjistri — the ones who have given me so much, the ones who I trusted — you say that they have deceived me.'

58

The Doctor laid a comforting hand on Miríl's shoulder. He knew what the older man was going through: the beliefs on which he had based his entire life were being cruelly undermined. Once, an unimaginably long time ago, the Doctor too had gone through a similar crisis of faith.

'I'm afraid so, Miríl.' The Doctor's voice was kind.

For many long moments Miríl did not speak. When he did, his tone was hard and flat, uncomprehending. 'What you say cannot be true, Doctor. The Panjistri are our benefactors. They saved us from barbarity and helped us to progress without war, strife and struggle.'

'And in doing so quenched whatever spirit you had in you, lowered your expectations of life. You obey blindly, Miríl, because it's easier that way.' The Doctor grabbed Miríl by the shoulders and stared intently into his eyes. 'Look deep inside yourself, Miríl. Tell me truthfully that you're happy.'

'I have all I want ... I have my books, my sustenance, my friendships ...'

'But are you happy?'

Miríl did not reply.

'Join me, Miríl,' urged the Doctor. 'Help me find out what the Panjistri are up to.'

Still Miríl did not reply. The Doctor played his trump card.

'I'm offering you the chance to be unhappy, Miríl, I want you never to be sure of what the future will bring. I want you to know how it feels to be hungry and I want you to experience the satisfaction of digging your own food from out of the ground. I want to offer you knowledge that you can't understand, and tell you of things you could never possibly achieve.

'I'm offering you frustration and despair and hardship, and that irreplaceable sense of triumph when you finally win against all the odds. I want you to know failure, and

59

realize that even in failing you succeed.

'I'm giving you the chance to be dependent on no one but yourself; the chance to make your own mistakes but to know that even if you can't reach the stars *at least you tried*!'

Miríl remained silent, but the look in his eyes told the Doctor that he had won his battle. There was a hardness in them now, a burning hate, and an immovable sense of purpose. The Doctor had seen that look only once before: and Alexander had gone on to conquer half a world.

But when Miríl did finally speak there was a certain sadness in his voice, the sadness of a child who cannot understand a complicated lesson, no matter how hard he tries.

'I am an old man, Doctor, and half my life has already passed me by. I have lived in this town for two hundred and fifty years, and the books and records in the library have taught me a great deal. When certain things troubled me, when I noted inconsistencies in the records, or gaps in my learning, I would push them to the back of my mind. If I did ask questions the Panjistri would always explain. But there is one question I would never ask.'

As he looked down at the Doctor there were tears in the old man's eyes. His lips trembled. 'I remember entering the seminary, Doctor, but before that my life is a blank.' His voice was pleading now. 'Why do I not remember my youth, Doctor, why do I not remember my childhood? Why do I not remember my parents?'

And the Doctor shuddered, as a frightening new suspicion dawned on him.

It was worse than playing hide and seek, thought Ace as Raphael avoided her for the second time that day. She had first seen him after her confrontation with Revna, a worried look on his face; he had walked quickly past her and vanished down one of the winding streets near the Council House. He had apparently not heard her calling after him.

So she'd returned to the seminary where Tanyel too had warned her off seeing Raphael: he'd always been something of a wild spirit, the older woman had said, and surely Ace would see that it was much wiser not to corrupt him with her alien ways. At which Ace had called the female Teacher an uncooperative old bag, leaving her speechless and fuming, and obtained Raphael's home address from a younger seminarian who had watched the entire confrontation with a mixture of horror and amusement.

Ace had never run after anyone in her life before; but if both Revna and Tanyel had warned her off Raphael, and if Raphael himself was now behaving so mysteriously, she was determined to find out why. Besides, the Professor himself had suggested that she get to know him better, and that was good enough for her. And that was her main reason for hunting him down, wasn't it?

Raphael lived in one of several small purpose-built apartment blocks near the gates of the town. Ace noted wryly that these were a far cry from the concrete monstrosities in and around Perivale — like everything else in Kirith these blended in perfectly with the architectural style of the surrounding buildings. These were flats for people to live in and not simply to exist on a meagre income and government handouts. When she rapped at Raphael's door there was no answer. She did however see a shadow sneaking out of a side entrance, but before she had time to pursue it, it had vanished round a corner.

She stamped her foot in irritation as the door to the neighbouring flat slid open. A young man, as handsome and as beautifully dressed as all the others on Kirith, looked at her curiously. 'If you're looking for Raphael he isn't there,' he said.

'Do you know where he might be then?'

'At this time of day he usually goes for a walk on the moors outside the town,' was the answer and the young man indicated the vague direction. 'Although I can't understand why he wants to do domething as boring and unproductive as that. You'll find him easily enough — no one else goes there.'

Ace thanked him and turned to go.

She became aware that the young man was looking her up and down, appraising her like one might a new animal at the zoo. He adopted a suggestive stance. 'Don't waste your time looking for crazy Raphael,' he said. 'I know of much better ways to spend the day.'

The implication was obvious, and Ace sighed, more out of boredom than outrage. What was wrong with this crazy town? If the women in this town weren't insulting her and accusing her of corrupting their youth, then the men were giving her the come-on.

'No thanks,' she chirped. 'Why don't you just start without me?'

She smiled her most charming smile, and skipped off, leaving the crestfallen young man wondering whether he ought to feel humiliated, insulted, or a mixture of the two.

It took the planet Kirith precisely sixteen and a quarter hours to spin once on its axis. By the time Ace had negotiated the winding streets and steep steps which led down the hill to the boundary walls, twilight was already falling. As she made her way through the open gates she was aware of the occasional passer-by staring disapprovingly at her. If she had looked up at the window set high in one of the turrets of the wall, she would have seen Revna watching her with hatred in her eyes.

Once outside the town and on the moors it was relatively easy to find Raphael. As the thwarted Romeo had said,

Raphael was the only moving object out there.

When Ace finally reached him he was sitting on a hillock, arms clasping his legs, looking up at the stars. He beamed when he saw her approach. She came and sat down next to him.

'How's the bruises?' she asked awkwardly.

'Fine,' he said. 'But Ace, you shouldn't be here.'

'Why not?'

'I can't be seen with you. Huldah doesn't approve.'

'Old slime-pants?' Ace said scornfully. Raphael was wide-eyed at her impudence. 'And do you always do what he says?'

'Well, not always ...' He smiled, remembering the escapades of his childhood, which had shocked half the town. Most of his pranks even then, he seemed to recall, had been directed at Huldah. But the memory of his childhood recalled Darien and the threat Huldah had made. He shuddered.

'Ace, you have to leave here,' he urged. 'You're upsetting everything Huldah and the Panjistri have striven to achieve.'

Ace looked at him quizzically, and he continued: 'You must have noticed the effect you're having on everyone.'

'Yeah,' she nodded, 'now I know how the monkeys in the zoo feel. I've not seen one friendly face yet — just a bunch of pretty plastic people staring at me.' Ignoring Raphael's protest she continued: 'This place is well weird. It's about as exciting as Sunday morning's telly. If it were up to me I'd leave right way.'

'And why don't you?'

'The Professor,' she explained, and fell silent. Since they had landed the Doctor hadn't said a word about their mission. He'd simply gone off on his own and urged her to get to know Raphael. And what's more she was doing just that. What was the Professor up to?

'He's an old friend,' she explained in answer to Raphael's unspoken question. 'My best friend.'

'And did you meet him in ... Peri-vale?' He pronounced the word awkwardly.

Ace laughed. 'No, somewhere a long way from there, somewhere up there.' She pointed up at the night sky, noticing for the first time just how few stars there were in the sky.

Raphael's eyes followed her finger. 'I come to this place a lot,' he said in wonder. 'Just to look at the stars ... If only I could get out there and touch them ... Tell me what it's like out there, Ace.'

She sighed. 'Fantastic. I love it. It's like one big ocean, and you're just a tiny drop of water in it. The freedom and all that space. You can look into it and know that even in a million years you wouldn't know one quarter of it, or what it's going to do next.' She turned and looked seriously at Raphael. 'I don't think there's anything which could make me leave it.'

'But don't you miss your friends, and your family?'

Ace froze. 'The Doctor's the only family I have now, OK? No one else matters.'

'I just thought −'

'Well, don't − OK?'

'My parents died when I was young. I never really knew them,' he explained. 'Since I was fourteen Miríl brought me up and taught me everything I know. But Miríl's an old man ...'

'But you have friends your own age. What about Revna?' Ace ventured.

Raphael snorted with amusement. 'Revna! She's just like all the others: follows all the rules, does everything Huldah and the Brethren tell her. Where's the fun in that?'

'Perhaps she's getting into practice for being a miserable old cow like Tanyel,' Ace suggested boldly. A conspiratorial look passed between the two and they both burst out laughing.

Then Raphael stopped abruptly and looked strangely into Ace's eyes. She flinched; the attention made her uncomfortable.

'Ace, you're different from anyone else in Kirith − I think I can trust you.'

'What is it, Raphael?'

'I had a friend once. His name was Darien ...'

As Raphael and Ace sat talking, they were unaware that their conversation was being overheard. Neither of them had ever seen the creature before but it had seen them: its presence had disturbed Raphael at the water's edge the previous night, and it had observed with wonder and eagerness the materialization of the TARDIS that same night.

If either Ace or Raphael could have seen the creature, its appearance would have terrified them: that was one of the reasons why it only ever ventured from its home under cover of darkness.

Hidden behind a clump of lush vegetation, away from the moonlight, it listened to Raphael telling Ace of his nightmares, and to Ace telling Raphael of the Doctor. It nodded silently to itself and there was a spark of eagerness in its hooded eyes.

When Ace and Raphael stood up to go, it wrapped its ragged cloak around itself and, still undetected, slinked soundlessly away towards the black range of hills to the west of the town, to the poisoned, forbidden realm which the Kirithons called the Darkfell and which it called home.

There would be much to tell its fellow exiles.

Chapter 7

'There is a great evil about,' the Doctor mused aloud to Ace the following morning, after she had told him of Raphael's nightmares. 'An entire race, forgetting their own past and meekly accepting whatever is given to them. Millions of years of evolution compressed into a few centuries. And behind it all, somehow, the Panjistri, like grandmasters, playing with the Kirithons as if they're pawns.' He paced the room, repeatedly hitting his fist into his open palm. 'What's the point of it all, Ace, what's the purpose?'

Ace shrugged. 'I told you there was something wrong about the whole set-up, didn't I? Even the weather's having an identity crisis.'

The Doctor looked through the window of Ace's room. The warm sunshine of the previous day had now given way to bleak wintry skies and biting winds. The Doctor shook his head despairingly. 'Climatic changes like this just shouldn't happen ... Did you see the Darkfell last night?'

Ace shook her head, and the Doctor elaborated. 'Miríl pointed it out to me. It's a range of hills a few miles to the west of here, poisoned and riddled with pollution, so he says. It glows, Ace.'

'Bad case of the Sellafield blues?'

The Doctor took a small Geiger counter out of one of his pockets. 'If it is radiation, it's of a kind that doesn't show up on this.'

'So what do we do now?'

'There's something happening on this planet that I don't understand. I want to know what it is. But we must tread carefully. Tanyel doesn't trust me: she's only allowing me to run free because of Miríl. And I suspect this Lord Huldah is only waiting for an opportunity to get us out of the way without any blame falling on him.'

'What do you want me to do?'

'Somehow Raphael's the key to all this: he's the only one who's remembering things he's not supposed to. Stay with him, find out what else he can remember about his friend — what's his name?'

'Darien.'

'Yes. If we can find what happened to him then we're halfway to an answer. And Ace.'

'Yes, Professor?'

The Doctor winked knowingly at her. 'Try not to make Revna even more jealous than she already is.'

'She's got no reason to be —' Ace's cheeks reddened at the Doctor's suggestion.

The Doctor raised a disbelieving eyebrow. 'No?'

She quickly changed the subject. 'And what are you going to do, Professor?'

'I,' said the Doctor with enthusiasm, 'I am going rock-climbing!'

Raphael was waiting for Ace on the rocks by the seashore, not far from where the TARDIS had landed. He was wearing a long furry coat to protect him from the biting winds. As she approached he jumped nervously to his feet;

when he saw who it was he relaxed.

'You sure this is OK?' asked Ace.

He nodded. 'It'll be safe to talk. No one ever comes down here.'

No one, that was, except Revna. And she had followed Ace at a discreet distance ever since she left the town this morning. She cursed through clenched teeth as she saw Raphael welcome her rival. Quickly she hid herself behind a large rock, and strained to hear their conversation above the whine of the wind.

Raphael took Ace's hand and led her up on to the rocks, steadying her when she slipped on the seaweed and shale. From this vantage point he pointed out to sea.

Ace pulled her windswept hair out of her eyes and gazed at the rocky island about a mile out to sea: squinting in the sunlight, she could make out a few tall trees, and a group of buildings in the centre of the island.

'So that's Kandasi,' she said, clearly unimpressed.

'The home of the Panjistri; it's where Darien was sent.'

'And you think he's still there?'

Raphael shrugged. 'I thought of swimming there once. I got into the most terrible trouble ...'

'It's probably more than anyone else would have done. But don't you have boats?'

'Only for freshwater fishing. The Panjistri forbid us to sail on the sea; it's —'

' "For your own protection",' she mimicked. 'Have you ever thought it might be for the Panjistri's protection?'

'Be fair, Ace,' he protested, unable to dismiss twenty-four years of indoctrination in one night. 'They provide us with so many things and forbid us so few: sea travel, the Darkfell, entry to the Harbours —'

'The Harbours?'

Raphael indicated a small tree-lined bay about half a mile along the coastline. 'It's where the Panjistri disembark when they visit us from Kandasi.'

'Well, that's just what we need!'

Raphael looked puzzled.

Ace sighed. 'Do I have to spell it out for you?'

Raphael noded. 'Yes, please.'

Ace raised her eyes heavenwards. 'Some Christopher Columbus you'd make! We sneak into the Harbours, wait until one of their boats pulls in, and then hide on board.'

'But —'

Ace cut him dead. 'Do you want to know what happened to your friend, or don't you?'

Raphael nodded uncertainly.

'So are you with me or not?'

Raphael looked out at Kandasi, and then back to Kirith town; and beyond that to the mysterious and forbidden Darkfell.

And then to the young woman who had saved his life and in whom he felt some strange kindred spirit; the young woman who had already upset the lives of many of his friends and was even now daring to break one of the most closely observed rules of all Kirith.

But it wasn't her inconoclasm that fascinated him, not her energy, not even her less than perfect beauty. Beneath her unpredictable and at times aggressive exterior, there was a tremendous amount of fun and a desire to live life to the fullest. And Raphael — and all of Kirith — had not lived life to the full for such a long time.

He took a deep breath, scarcely realizing what he was committing himself to.

'I'm with you, Ace.'

Revna had heard enough. Her eyes smarting with tears she would not allow to fall, she made her way quickly back to the Lord Huldah.

Long, long ago, even before the Panjistri came to Kirith,

a great race dwelt on the planet. They were men of vast abilities and great learning. They were also accomplished architects and builders and raised magnificent buildings and temples to their gods.

But as the ages passed, so they were consumed with greed and envy of their fellow man. Conflicts broke out between rival towns, wars were declared between continents, and hideous engines of destruction were built.

Within decades the original Kirithons had become extinct, having wiped themselves out with their own death machines. Even today, the Darkfell was still blighted with their poisons. But their buildings survived, touched only by the uncaring passage of time. To the new species which arose on Kirith, these ruins stood as a reminder of the barbarity and futility of war.

One such ruin lay a few miles inland from Kirith town. When Miríl had told him about its existence the Doctor had shown a keen interest in seeing them for himself; perhaps in the ruins of the past he would find the answers which the records on Kirith concealed.

The Doctor looked up uncertainly at the ruins, which lay isolated about halfway up a steep rocky tor. 'It's a long way up,' he said without much enthusiasm. 'Are you sure you're up to it, Miríl?'

Miríl looked hurt. 'I am only two hundred and fifty years old, Doctor; I'm not yet ready for retirement,' he reminded him. 'And it might be ... amusing.'

'Of course,' said the Doctor, and smiled knowingly. 'You know, Miríl, I suspect you were a bit of a tearaway in your younger days. Not dissimilar to our young friend Raphael, in fact?'

'I raised Raphael as my ward from the age of fourteen,' Miríl said, neatly avoiding the question. 'Now may I suggest that we start to climb?'

A pathway of sorts twisted its way halfway up the tor

and so the initial part of the journey proved not particularly difficult. From that point, however, it became steeper and the two men found themselves having to look out for footholds and projecting rocks which they would use to haul themselves up.

For a man of his age Miríl was surprisingly nimble, and more than once he had to stop to help the Doctor. The Doctor accepted the assistance begrudgingly. It was all right for Miríl, he thought ruefully: this wasn't the first time he had made the trip, he suspected. And besides, he was a Time Lord, not a blessed mountain goat!

Occasionally they would trip and stumble on loose stones, or the wind would blow them slightly off balance. Because the tor ascended by a series of small plateaux they weren't in danger of their lives; but a fall down to the previous ledge could still result in broken limbs.

After about half an hour's climbing they stopped to rest on a large overhanging ledge: some twenty feet above them was the summit. Looking enviously at Miríl, who didn't seem in the slightest tired, the Doctor paused to catch his breath and to take a look at the surrounding area.

He took a small brass telescope out of a pocket of his duffle coat; Miríl looked at it with fascination. The Doctor offered it to him; he put the wrong end to his eye before the Doctor corrected him with a smile.

'An invention of an Italian friend of mine,' he said airily.

From this vantage point he could see that Kirith town and its immediate environs were effectively cut off from the rest of the countryside. The tor on which they were standing was to the south of Kirith town and formed one of the foothills of a vast range of mountains which, Miríl said, spanned the entire continent.

To the west and the east ran two rivers, one of which provided fresh water for the town, the other of which flowed through the Darkfell, still forbidding and inscrutable even in the daylight. Further to the east was the bay which Miríl called the Harbours of the Chosen and, beyond that, a dense forest of tall dark trees.

And, as always, out in the northern seas, the brooding watchful presence of Kandasi Island.

Miríl handed the telescope back to the Doctor, who insisted that he keep it, suggesting he could use it to look at the stars.

Miríl thanked him effusively. 'It is indeed a wonderful device, Doctor,' he said with awe. 'You must tell me how to make one.'

'I've no doubt your computers could tell you — if you could program them correctly,' he replied, and continued to look thoughtfully out at Kandasi.

So intent was the Doctor in looking seawards that he failed to notice the tell tale sign of stones and small rocks skittering and falling down the steep sides of the tor.

Miríl dived at the Doctor, striking him in the small of the back and sending him flying towards the edge of the ledge. A massive boulder came thundering down the side of the tor, smashing down on to the very spot where the Doctor had been standing just a moment before.

It crashed to a halt for a second before tumbling off the side of the ledge and continuing to roll down to the ground some hundred feet below.

The already fragile ledge had been weakened by the impact, and began to crack and crumble.

As the ledge tottered over into space the Doctor frantically clawed his way to securer ground. His legs hung over the edge, waving frantically in the winds; his hat was knocked off his head and floated down to the ground.

With one hand grabbing hold of some hardy shrubs for support, Miríl reached out with his other hand for the Doctor. Their fingers met, and with aching and straining muscles Miríl pulled the Doctor away from the edge.

The Doctor sat up, an undignified mess, and wiped at a small cut above his eye with a handkerchief.

'Thank you, Miríl,' he said breathlessly.

Miríl just smiled. 'It was purely a selfish act, Doctor,' he said. 'After all, I couldn't let all your knowledge go to waste, could I?'

'Nevertheless, thank you.' The Doctor shaded his eyes from the sun and looked up at the top of the tor. 'Boulders don't just dislodge themselves and fall like that,' he said. 'I think someone doesn't want us to reach the top, Miríl.'

Miríl frowned. A few days ago he could not even have contemplated the idea that there were people on Kirith prepared to deceive and to kill their fellow men; now it was beginning to seem a commonplace.

'So what do we do now, Doctor?'

'Why, we go over the top, of course!'

'Have you never wished for the peaceful life, Doctor?' Miríl sighed.

The Doctor shook his head and chuckled. 'Lots of people have asked me that. It's much more fun my way.'

Dusting himself off, he stood up to begin the final climb.

Ten minutes later the Doctor and Miríl had reached the summit of the tor.

The wind whistled through the shattered skeletons of buildings, and toppled pillars and piles of rubble littered the ground — the ruins of what had once been a small settlement and lookout post to sea. The Doctor bent down and picked up a handful of ash; he let it slip slowly through his fingers.

This ash was, after all, the unavoidable result of each and every war; if the Panjistri had indeed saved the Kirithons from this horror did he really have the right to interfere?

He stood up and looked around sadly. And then he

frowned: surely something wasn't quite right here? 'How long have these ruins been here, Miríl?'

'Five or six thousand years. They are all that remain of the original inhabitants of our planet. We leave them here as a lesson that we should never misuse our technology the way they misused theirs.'

The Doctor fumbled in his pockets and took out a small device, roughly the size and shape of a pocket calculator. 'It's a radiation detector, among other things,' he explained to Miríl, as he clicked it on and began walking among the destroyed buildings. When he returned his brow was creased with concern; he tapped the device as if to ensure that it was functioning properly.

'What's wrong, Doctor?'

'In this area between five and six thousand years ago there was a terrible nuclear war?'

'The original Kirithons split the atom, yes.'

'So even now this place should be steeped in some residual radiation.'

The Doctor drew Miríl's attention to the radiation detector. 'There isn't even the slightest trace of radiation, natural or unnatural. The only radiation anywhere on this entire planet is artron energy.' Miríl looked at him blankly as he continued. 'And I now know exactly where it's coming from.'

'Where, Doctor?'

The Doctor snorted angrily. 'Where do you think?'

The two men gazed out at Kandasi Island.

The Doctor turned away disgustedly and looked back at the ruins. 'There's more than one sort of radiation this little device can detect,' he said as he jabbed at several further buttons. 'There's one more test I want to make. It won't be as effective as a laboratory experiment, but it will tell me what I need to know.'

He passed the device over the dead husk of a tree, which

had been felled when a pillar had fallen on top of it. For a few second the detector buzzed and whirred and then beeped its conclusions on to a tiny LCD screen.

With a sense of bitter triumph the Doctor showed the results to Miríl.

'What have you done, Doctor?'

'A rudimentary carbon-14 test,' he answered, and when Miríl looked blank added: 'Something they would never teach you. It's designed to give an approximate age to any organic structure.'

'And what does it tell you?'

'I rather suspect you've already guessed, Miríl,' the Doctor said. 'Six thousand years, you say? More like six hundred! Like the library records, those ruins are a fake, a sop to make you think you had a history, and a warning to you not to develop technology that might one day threaten the Panjistri.

'There never was a war; there never was another race on this planet − this world is much too young and sterile to support intelligent life anyway.'

Miríl's eyes blazed with curiosity and an unexpected delight. 'You mean we're not Kirithons? That we come from . . . from the stars?' Did this explain his fascination with the heavens, wondered Miríl; was it because his race was actually born out there in that great void?

'This whole planet is a giant crucible,' continued the Doctor, 'and the Kirithons are part of some evil experiment that was begun here long ago. Miríl, the experiment must stop!'

As the Doctor and Miríl began their descent down to the ground, Huldah moved out of the ruined building in which he had been hiding. His attempt to kill the Doctor with the boulder had failed, but with what the Doctor now knew it was even more imperative that he be disposed of.

Nothing could be allowed to interfere with the task of

the Panjistri, especially now that the Omega Point was so close.

Yet even as he plotted ways to rid himself of the Doctor, the Lord Procurator Huldah allowed himself a small self-satisfied smile. The Time Lord was a genius, certainly; but Huldah knew something that even he didn't.

The Doctor was wrong, fatally wrong. For the Kirithons were very much natives of this planet. Both they and the world on which they lived had been created for one very special and overriding purpose.

And he, Huldah, alone on all Kirith, knew what that purpose was.

Although the Harbours were only a half a mile along the coast, it took Ace and Raphael over two hours to reach them. As they approached the bay, the rocky coastline rose to high unscaleable cliffs and the pair were forced to travel inland through dense woods. When they arrived it was late afternoon. They stood at the top of a small hill and looked down into the bay below.

If there was anything to contrast with Kirith town, thought Ace, then this was it.

Whereas Kirith in all its Gothic splendour buzzed with sumptuous life, the Harbours were cold and dead. Nothing grew here, apart from a few shrubs struggling to survive; even the trees near the shore were bare and charred.

The only sound was the sea as it crashed against the rocks on the shore, and the wind whistling through the bleakness and desolation. Otherwise, a shroud of silence hung over the place. If the Doctor had been there he would have recognized it at once for what it was: the silence of death, the same silence that hangs over Auschwitz and Treblinka.

Several drab and windowless buildings stood along the sea edge. Grey and functional, little more than large concrete boxes, they reminded Ace of old abandoned military bases. Four watchtowers surrounded the base but they were unmanned: obviously the Kirithons' unquestioning obedience made their use unnecessary.

For a moment the pair stood silently, until Ace remembered what they had come here for. She looked seawards, but no boats were moored in the bay.

'Let's just go back then,' said Raphael a little too eagerly: he'd no wish to stay here a moment longer than necessary.

Ace looked at him with undisguised contempt. 'Not on your life.'

On the way Raphael had told her that though the Panjistri were infrequent visitors to Kirith town, they visited the Harbours on a regular basis: for what purpose no one knew. Ace intended to wait until they came.

In the meantime she was going to explore the base: it was high time that she found out what was really happening on this planet. She began to make her way down towards the buildings; then she turned and looked at Raphael.

'Well, are you coming or not?'

Raphael hesitated and then, accepting the inevitable, followed Ace down the hill.

As they approached the buildings they could see no sign of life at all, not even refuse or discarded machinery. Everything was ordered and precise, as though the base had not been used for years.

Each of the buildings had a large rusted iron door. With a nervous Raphael in tow Ace tried every one of them. All were locked.

'There's nothing here, Ace; let's get back.'

'No way, sunshine,' she said, and slung her rucksack off her back.

'What are you doing?'

She grinned. 'Causing a few hiccoughs in Paradise. Now stand back.'

She opened her bag and took out what to Raphael appeared to be two cans of female deodorant. She placed them by the door of a small cement hut, took off their caps, and stood back, bumping into Raphael, who had ignored her advice and was watching over her shoulder.

'Get back, will you!' she shouted.

She pushed him down as the two cans of nitro-nine exploded with a deafening roar, blowing the iron door inwards.

'Wicked!' cried Ace. 'Not very ozone friendly of course, but you can't have everything.'

Raphael just lay on the floor, shocked beyond belief: no one else was anything like Ace. His mouth was open wide in amazement. Ace leant down and obligingly shut it for him.

'Are they all like you in Peri-vale?' he gulped.

'Nah, some of them are really violent,' she said. 'Now let's see what we've got here.'

To their surprise the building was empty. Steps led down below ground. Ace took a flashlight out of her bag and urged Raphael to follow.

'Wow! Hammer Horror!' whistled Ace, as they reached the bottom after about five minutes' descent. 'It's like something out of a Frankenstein movie.'

A vast laboratory had been set up in an underground cavern. Row upon row of workbenches, cluttered with specimen jars and scientific equipment whose use they could only guess at, filled the vast cavern.

Along one rock wall computers whirred, automatically analysing and processing data. A series of empty barred cages lined the opposite wall.

Another wall was almost completely taken up with an enormous screen upon which columns and rows of numbers and formulae and complex three-dimensional graphic designs flashed with staggering rapidity. Ace could make neither head nor tail of any of them.

High above their heads a maze of transparent pipes criss-crossed, carrying viscous liquids which were fed into a large vat at the far end of the cavern. Huge monitors hung from the ceiling, displaying moving geometric patterns which pulsed and reconfigured themselves to a heartbeat rhythm. In spite of several ventilation shafts which buzzed noisily, a noxious, familiar smell pervaded the entire cavern.

Raphael looked around in amazement. 'This is what the Panjistri do here? But what's it all for?'

Ace strode over to one of the workbenches. She screwed up her face in disgust as she looked at some of the specimen jars. 'Horrible stuff,' she muttered to herself.

Each of the specimen jars was filled with a perfectly preserved human or animal embryo, and Ace now recognized the ubiquitous smell as formaldehyde. Not all the specimens were fully developed; some were little more than small glutinous masses of cells.

On another workbench three grey heavy lumps floated in tanks of effervescent fluid into which had been inserted copper electrodes. Meters by the side of the jars recorded any neurological activity in the brains as charges of electricity were pulsed through them. In a corner, two disembodied hearts pumped away in a tank of foul-smelling nutrients.

Looking up at one of the monitors Ace recognized a graphic representation of the dual ribbons of the DNA molecule, the building block of life.

'They're biologists,' she said.

'What?'

'Didn't they teach you biology at school?' she asked, already knowing the answer before Raphael had the chance to shake his head.

'This is were Darien came?' asked Raphael.

Ace shrugged; she didn't like to think of the answer. These specimens, after all, had to come from somewhere and she would bet that the Panjistri wouldn't donate their own precious organs for the sake of their experiments.

She took a disk off a desk and inserted it into a wall-mounted computer. For a second the computer whirred, processing the data, and then the monitor was filled with a sequence of stylized images.

A small dot flickered alone in the centre of the screen. Steadily it grew until it exploded, sending dots and beams of light out into every direction like an incredible firework display. Almost faster than the eye could see, they raced out until the entire screen was covered with the tiny moving pinpricks of light.

And then, imperceptibly at first, their progess slowed until they came to a halt. For a full half-minute there was no movement on the screen. Then, at first slowly and then ever faster, the beams of light fell in upon themselves, drawing closer and closer to their centre, until there was nothing left on the screen but the original bright pinprick of light. And then it too blipped out of existence, leaving only the silent blackness of the computer screen.

Ace dimly recognized the pattern she had just seen. But before she could remember she heard a strained whisper behind her.

'Ace . . .'

While she had been looking at the screen Raphael had wandered off to a small room set apart from the main laboratory. Through its open doorway pulsed a cold unearthly blue light. Ace followed the sound of his voice and felt herself gag as a stench like that of dead and rotting fish filled the air.

In the centre of the room stood a huge transparent, open-topped cylinder, about nine feet high, into which several pumps fed blue nutrient fluid. A tangle of wires ran off from the cylinder to digital display meters set in the far wall.

Thrashing about in the tank was a creature from a nightmare.

Its bulbous head, overdeveloped in comparison to the rest of its body, reminded Ace of nothing more than a monstrously overgrown foetus. But there all resemblance to the human form ended.

Suspended in the blue-green liquid, its limbs — Ace counted eight in all — splayed from its underdeveloped torso and jerked about, some battering at the walls of the cylinder which imprisoned it, some reaching upwards for the oxygen-rich air above it. Some were small and weak, little more than scrawny sticks of gristle; others were strong and well developed, their six-fingered hands clenching and flexing reflexively.

Part of its stomach was open and long tubular organs covered with a thick mucus poured out of it, swaying back and forth, as the creature turned and twisted, writhing in its own excrement, blood and vomit.

Parts of its lungs and twin hearts were exposed too, and they expanded and contracted, breathing in the life-giving nutrient all around it.

Several oversized eyes protruded from its skull, each of them looking in different directions, blinking in the harsh light of the laboratory. The creature had no ears, but a small ineffectual lipless mouth constantly opened and closed, fishlike, gulping greedily at the life-giving fluid which surrounded it.

When it saw Ace and Raphael its eyes fixed them with a baleful stare and its mouth let out a hideous blood-curdling screech, like the caw of a trapped and tortured bird holding them responsible for its present situation.

It moved its head with difficulty; electrodes, connected to a bank of meters outside the cylinder, restricted its movements considerably. Small copper-plated conductors, attached to generators at the far end of the room, punctuated the cylinder, sending short flashes of energy through the creature's body.

For the split second that its body was lit up and suffused with energy its nerves and nascent, pliable bones became visible. Each time the energy bolts coursed through its body it screamed in torment, twisting and convulsing, and globs of flesh and guts would detach themselves from its body to float in the oily fluid.

The world spun sickeningly around Ace and she turned away; to her utter disgust she found herself throwing up. A white-faced Raphael was by her side in an instant; she pushed him away.

'I'm all right,' she snapped, and forced herself to look at the creature in the tank. The creature returned her stare with the fear and hate given to anything that is different.

'They're breeding it,' she said incredulously. 'Creating it out of mutated cells and dead organs.'

'What is it?' asked Raphael.

'Your salvation.'

The two turned around, and Raphael gripped Ace's arm tightly. 'Lord Reptu!' he gasped.

Reptu shook his head sadly and looked down at them; his weak eyes regarded them sternly, like a disappointed headmaster reproving two wayward students.

'The Homunculus is the first of an entirely new species,' he said. 'A creature of infinite aggression, created especially to be the saviour of your race, Raphael; indeed, of all races.'

'It's horrible,' cried Ace. 'Obscene.'

Raphael urged her to be quiet and show due respect. 'Ace, he's a Panjistri,' he hissed.

Ace shook herself away from his arm. 'I don't care who he is, I want some explanations.' She poked at Reptu with her finger. 'What's going on here, Granddad?'

To her fury Reptu just smiled as one would to a capricious child; if anything, her anger and aggression seemed to delight him.

'You will find out soon, Earthchild; both you and the Doctor are part of our great plan.'

Ace caught the threat in his voice and a thrill of terror ran down her spine. She pushed past the old man, who did nothing to stop her, and called Raphael to follow her.

Reptu snapped his fingers and from out of the shadows lumbered six Companions, brothers to Fetch. Their teeth were bared threateningly and they slavered and snarled as they circled Ace and Raphael like cats stalking their prey.

'There is no escape for either of you now,' said Reptu flatly. 'Now that you have been here you have no choice but to join our Brotherhood.' He turned to Ace. 'It is your destiny.'

'My Lord, we meant no harm,' Raphael pleaded, his Kirithon upbringing once again superseding Ace's influence. 'Let us go, and your secrets are safe with us.'

'Like hell they are,' cried Ace, and grabbed Raphael's arm. 'I'm not ending up like that thing. Come on!'

Dragging Raphael with her, she tried to barge past the Companions. They closed in on her, their claws pawing at her body, tearing at her jacket. Shocked into action, Raphael tried to stop them, only to be swatted aside like an irritating insect. The Companions' sole concern was Ace.

She shrugged of her backpack, and raised it above her head, swinging it around like a club. The Companions backed away and Ace seized her chance, diving through the opening in the circle, pulling Raphael after her.

As the band of Companions followed them, Ace swept the contents of a workbench to the floor. Several burettes smashed on to the floor, releasing noxious fumes into the air and sending the Companions, with their acute sense of smell, into fits of coughing and spluttering.

'Get after them!' cried Reptu, his entire body shaking with rage and frustration. 'Everything depends on the girl!'

Delayed by the fumes for only seconds, one of the Companions leapt after them, grabbing Ace's backpack and knocking both it and her down to the ground. Raphael snatched the bag and swung it full into the creature's face. With a yelp of pain it backed away, blood streaming from its snout.

Ace and Raphael ran out of the laboratory, upsetting workbenches and containers on the way to impede further their pursuers' progress. As a Companion came close, Ace swung at it with her heavy flashlight. Their hearts pumping furiously, they climbed the steps leading up to the outside.

Caught up in the thrill of the hunt, the Companions reverted to the animals they had once been. Growling and baying they snapped angrily at Ace and Raphael's heels.

Outside night had fallen. Clouds obscured the moons and it was pitch black. Seeking refuge behind a building Ace turned to Raphael.

'Go!' she panted. 'They can't hunt both of us. It's me they want, not you.'

He shook his head violently.

'Listen, I've not got time for arguing! Find the Professor. Tell him what's happening.'

Nearby they heard the Companions exiting the building, pausing to sniff at the wind for their scent.

'Ace, I can't leave you!'

'Get lost, Raphael! Save yourself!'

With a bay of triumph the Companions detected their presence. As one hungry herd they raced towards their prey.

Chapter 8

Where is the warm nothingness that was so comforting?
Now there is nothing but harsh light and biting cold and
no possibility of ever going back.
    Only choice now — go forward and face the threat, face
the future.
    The future.
    The future is uncertain, and uncertainty worries me.
Scares me.
    What will happen? Will I survive?

Who is the other presence that haunts me, and threatens
me, and scares me, and shapes my future, and is my future,
and threatens my future, and guarantees my future.
    I am uncertain.
    He/She/It scares me.
    Is he/she/it aware of me? Is he/she/it scared too?
    I am uncertain.

Ace ran on, her legs aching with pain, and her panting
breath cutting her lungs like a knife. Behind her the
Companions pursued her relentlessly; it was only their
apparent inability to organize and act as a group which

had prevented them from capturing her so far.

Unlike Ace, they seemed never to tire: it would only be a matter of time before they reached her. Hiding behind a clump of trees in a small gully and pausing for breath, she cursed herself for panicking and running inland away from the Harbours instead of following the coast. Now she was hopelessly lost on the moors without Raphael, who had reluctantly followed her advice and run off on his own.

The starless night was pitch black. What little light there was to see by came from the twin moons overhead. Far off in the distance the lights of Kirith town twinkled and called: there would be the Doctor, she thought, and beyond that the warm security of the TARDIS.

A harsh rasping sound made her jump. Crouched above her a Companion stood, its teeth bared, it claws beckoning her. It leapt down into the gully. Ace backed nervously against a tree.

'My pretty,' it hissed, 'there is no escape: return to the Panjistri. Fulfil your destiny.'

'No chance!' she cried defiantly. With a strength which surprised even her she wrenched off a low hanging branch from the tree, and brought it crashing down on the creature's skull.

It howled in pain and stumbled away. Ace took her chance and scrambled up out of the gully. She looked wildly around. The other Companions had gone off in another direction; now was her chance to get back to the Doctor.

A spine-chilling howl rose from the gully; her attacker had recovered quickly and was calling to its brothers, alerting them of her whereabouts. Even now she could see them coming from the direction of the town.

There was only one way to run, towards the west. As she ran and ran, the baying of the Companions behind her, all sense of time and space was sublimated by her over-riding instinct for survival; it was only after ten or fifteen minutes that she realized her pursuers had stopped the chase.

She looked up. Before her stood the Darkfell, the place forbidden to all Kirithons. A dark wooded hill, it looked down on her impassively, seeming to offer her sanctuary. Its trees, creaking and waving in the wind, glowed with a ghostly blue phosphorescence.

Ace looked back at the Companions. They were cowering in groups, whimpering to each other. Some were even breaking away from the main body and heading back to the town.

They're scared of it, she suddenly realized.

'Come with us,' they cried. 'There lies death for you!'

'Accept the Panjistri; join the Brotherhood!'

Ace picked up a handful of stones which she threw at them. 'Bog off, wimps!' she taunted. 'Get back to your kennels!'

Forcing herself not to run, she quickly made her way up the hill. Behind her the Companions watched her with wary, frightened eyes.

When Raphael ran off from the Harbours a few of the Companions gave chase. Their hunt of him was half-hearted, however; as Ace had said, it wasn't him they were interested in. Raphael knew the moors well, and it was a simple matter to shake them off.

Nevertheless he didn't stop running or looking out for pursuers until he reached the safety of Kirith town. When he stopped he found he was trembling, not because of the chase, not even because of the horror he had seen in the laboratory. His whole world had been upset by the simple fact that the kindly, if stern, Lord Reptu, and the harmless Companions had now been shown in their true light.

87

He had to tell someone what he had discovered and find the Doctor. It was dangerous to return to his home now; Huldah would surely have been alerted of his crimes and Raphael remembered all too clearly the Lord Procurator's earlier threat.

So it was that he found himself standing at Revna's door in the middle of the night, Ace's backpack slung across his shoulder.

As always, Revna was still awake, working hard at papers she had brought from Huldah's offices. When she saw Raphael she expressed surprise which immediately turned to concern on seeing his ashen face. She led him to a chair.

'What happened?'

Raphael buried his face in his hands. 'It was horrible, Revna, like a giant deformed baby being torn apart.' There were tears in his eyes as he told her of his discovery in the laboratory. 'The Panjistri are doing terrible things, tampering with nature like that. We've got to stop them.'

Revna was bewildered, unable to make any sense of his words. She placed a tender hand on Raphael's shoulder. 'The Panjistri are our providers, Raphael,' she said softly. 'Our wellbeing and our sustenance all come from them.'

'But at what expense?' He shook his head and nodded to the window. 'It's not safe for me out there now. You must find the Doctor for me. Tell him everything. Ace is in trouble.'

Revna froze. When she replied there was a hard edge to her voice.

'You are wrong, Raphael. Whatever you've seen must be for our benefit. The Panjistri mean us no harm.' Then she seemed to relent. 'But if it's important to you I'll fetch the Doctor from the seminary.' Raphael smiled his appreciation. 'As for Ace, she wouldn't have got in this mess if she hadn't gone snooping around the Harbours in the first place.'

'How did you know where we went? I didn't tell you.'

Revna's face fell. 'Ace is a rogue element,' she said defensively, 'she's not part of our life here.'

Raphael pushed Revna away in disgust and stood up angrily. 'You informed on us.'

'I did it for you, Raphael. Ace is a bad influence on you —'

'In the past three days I've lived more than you have in the past twenty-eight years!' he raged. 'If that's a bad influence then I'm all for it.'

'I did it for you,' she repeated, tears now in her eyes.

'Well, don't. You've interfered with my life ever since we were children and I'm tired of it. I'm tired of you never questioning what's given to you, always keeping within the precious rules. I want to be with real people, not cold and efficient fawners like Tanyel and you.'

Revna found it an effort to keep her voice steady. 'My duty is to the smooth running of Kirith and the happiness of its citizens. We must all accept our responsibilities at some time, Raphael. We can't be children forever.'

'Can't we?' Raphael glared at her, and then threw Ace's rucksack over his shoulder and stormed out.

For minutes Revna sat silently, staring into space. She had always acted with Raphael's best interests in mind, she told herself; Ace and the Doctor were harmful influences on him and on all Kirith, and they needed to be disposed of.

But if Raphael was to reject her advice, that was up to him. Hard though it was to make the choice, she realized that her prime duty lay with Kirith, not with the one who had always rejected her advances.

And if it was no longer possible for Revna to love with passion, then she would hate with fury.

* * *

The Darkfell reminded Ace of the fairy-tale woods of her childhood books, full of dark and uncertain menace. Many of the trees were dead and barren; the others had grown to enormous heights, and their spreading branches concealed the sky. The trees and much of the vegetation glowed with an eerie phosphorescence.

Small animals skittered about, burrowing for insects in the ground or hiding in the grass at the sound of her approach. Patches of mist hung over small pools of foul-smelling water. The only sound was the wind whistling ghostlike through the trees.

She could see why the Companions hadn't followed her here. A sense of evil covered the place like a shroud, and there was that peculiar smell, like ammonia. Was that the poison Raphael had talked about?

She looked behind her and tensed. She could have sworn she saw a movement in the bushes. Cautiously she approached the spot: but there was nothing there.

This is crazy, she thought. I'm acting like Red Riding Hood looking for the wolf! But still she could not rid herself of a vague sense of unease, a suspicion that someone was watching her.

'Who's there?' she stammered.

No reply.

She quickened her pace. There was something there, she was sure of it. Panic set in and she fled the unseen threat, running into branches which scratched at her face and ripped at her jacket.

Reaching a clearing, she tripped over the root of a tree, twisting her ankle and crashing down to the ground. Wide-eyed with fear, she watched as dark shadows closed in on her from every side, taking advantage of her helplessness.

Well, at least I'll go down with a fight, she thought and grabbed at a small rock, raising her arm to throw it.

The creatures came closer and she froze with horror at the sight of them. The rock dropped from her hand.

They were dressed in rags and were recognizably humanoid. Yet these were humans whose like she had never seen before. They seemed incomplete, pathetic mockeries of the human form.

Many of them were armless, or legless, dragging themselves along the ground by their arms. Other had underdeveloped limbs, like ghastly thalidomide victims, while the arms of others were so long that they trailed apelike on the ground.

Some had male faces on otherwise female bodies; one had no face at all, just a blank mound of flesh. Another woman had a third eye in the middle of her forehead, and walked hand in hand with a man whose entire body was covered in coarse hair and who had no mouth.

They all muttered amongst themselves, pointing at Ace and shaking their heads.

Ace winced in terror as the band of freaks surrounded her. One of them, a male whose entire body was covered in crusty sores, reached out a gnarled hand to her.

She instinctively backed away in revulsion which quickly turned to amazement and incredulity.

The creature was tearing a strip of cloth off the rags he was wearing and binding her injured ankle. Despite the arthritic appearance of his hands he was performing the task with ease and great dexterity.

His companions looked on, making noises of appreciation at his skill.

After he had finished binding her ankle, he bared his yellowing teeth: it was, Ace decided, his approximation of a smile.

'Th-thank you,' she said.

The creature bowed his head. 'I assure you it was entirely my pleasure, young lady,' he said in a voice rich with plummy vowels. 'Let me help you to your feet.'

'You can speak!' Ace gasped in amazement, as she took hold of his hand.

'And why shouldn't he?' asked an imperious female voice. The crowd surrounding Ace parted to reveal the speaker.

Like the others she was dressed in rags, but even in these she walked tall and upright, as if they were the most regal robes ever fashioned. Her blue flesh was almost totally transparent and through it Ace could see nerves and blood vessels which pumped and pulsed as she spoke. Her silky hair was pulled tightly back, as though deliberately to draw attention to the cruel oozing sore on her forehead. Her scarred and mutilated face could not quite conceal her once-haughty beauty.

'We may look like animals and monsters but I assure you we were once as human as you.'

'I'm... I'm sorry, I didn't realize,' Ace replied guiltily.

'I am Arun, of the Unlike,' said the woman. 'What were you doing on the Darkfell? I thought it was forbidden to all Kirithons.'

'But I'm not a Kirithon —'

Arun took the information in her stride. 'So the Panjistri are still luring star travellers to this planet.' She touched Ace's face with a cold and clammy hand and looked at her more closely. 'Now I recognize you. I saw your arrival. The companion of the Doctor.'

'You know him?'

Arun shook her head. 'I know of him. The Panjistri have waited for his coming for centuries now, here at the end of all things.'

Ace looked puzzled, and Arun explained. 'The Universe is old and nearing its close. Aeons of expansion have exhausted its energies. Now stars are dying and the Universe itself is contracting and falling in on itself. In such circumstances the Panjistri believed the Doctor would have to come. But why they awaited him with such eagerness I never found out, even when I was in their service.'

'You worked for the Panjistri?'

'They trained me to be their assistant. I worked for them at the Harbours, on the breeding of the Homunculus —'

'You were responsible for that?' accused Ace.

'It was to my advantage,' Arun replied coldly. 'I'm a scientist. Only by working at the Harbours could I have access to all the technology that the Panjistri denied the other Kirithons.'

'It's disgusting.'

'Yes.'

'But why are they breeding it?'

'Who knows? It's better not to ask too many awkward questions of our great benefactors,' she said ironically, and indicated her face. 'When I began to investigate their actions this is what happened to me. The Panjistri are the greatest geneticists the Universe has ever known,' she said in reply to Ace's unspoken question. 'Over the centuries they've been using the Kirithons in their genetic experiments; the Homunculus was bred from cultivated Kirithon cells. A few are taken to Kandasi; the others are experimented on at the Harbours, subjected to the most hideous tortures in the name of science and curiosity. Even I could not tolerate that.' She waved a hand at her colleagues. 'We are all the results of the Panjistri's experiments, the unlucky ones who escaped from the Harbours and lived.'

'But why hasn't anyone stood up to them? Why hasn't anyone noticed their friends disappearing?'

Arun laughed bitterly. 'The Panjistri were once great telepaths; even now, with their powers diminished, they can influence conditioned minds. They provide Kirith with *zavát*, a marvellous source of sustenance and the base

93

constituent of all the food eaten on Kirith. It weakens the resistance centres of the brain and makes all but the strongest minds susceptible to telepathic suggestions.' She laughed bitterly. 'But if only the Kirithons knew what *zavát* really was.'

Ace shuddered, and felt herself wanting to retch as she recalled the food she had eaten during her stay in the seminary.

'*Zavát* is nothing more than the reconstituted remains of the victims of the Panjistri's genetic experiments. The Kirithons, if only they knew it, are eating their own kind.'

Dawn was breaking over Kirith town when Raphael found the Doctor and Miríl in the seminary library, debating their plan of action. Breathlessly Raphael began to tell the Doctor of his discovery at the Harbours, but the Doctor's first concern was for Ace.

'What do you mean, you left her?' he cried angrily.

'She made me,' he protested. 'Said it was her they were after, not me.'

The Doctor bit his lip to suppress his anger and concern. 'You were supposed to look after her, Jamie –'

Raphael and Miríl looked curiously at him. The Doctor clenched his fists in anger. 'Not Jamie, Raphael,' he reminded himself. Why did he keep slipping back to his old persona? What was his second incarnation trying to tell him? He took a few deep breaths.

'Things are getting too much out of control,' he said. 'Where might she have gone?'

Raphael shrugged guiltily.

The Doctor sighed. Ace could probably look after herself, he supposed, even without the contents of her backpack which Raphael was now carrying. Their first priority was to return to the Harbours, and then to Kandasi: it was time to confront the Panjistri on their home ground.

Miríl and Raphael viewed the prospect with gloom but reluctantly followed the Doctor as he stalked out of the library.

Abruptly he turned back. 'Miríl is there another way out of here?'

Miríl indicated a door at the furthest end of the room.

'Then I suggest that we use that.'

'Why?'

'Would a gang of baying overgrown weasels be a good enough reason?'

'Ah yes, I suppose so.'

They ran down the aisles of books and reading desks as Huldah and four Companions burst through the main door. Caught up once more in the thrill of the chase, the Companions leapt over desks and tables, overturning computers and piles of precious manuscripts in their effort to reach the Doctor and his party.

Raphael was the first to reach the second door and turned to see how his friends were doing.

Huldah confronted the Doctor, pushing him against one of the large bookshelves which lined the room. 'Surrender, Doctor, there is no chance of escape.'

'Oh, I don't know,' said the Doctor as his hands reached for the bookshelf behind him. 'A friend of mine once said that the pen is mightier than the sword, you know.'

'What are you talking about?' asked Huldah, and found out precisely what the Doctor was talking about when a heavy volume hit him full square in the belly, winding him.

The Companions were meanwhile playing a macabre game of cat and mouse with Miríl, chasing him round the long reading tables of the library, while the old man tried desperately to reason with them. Finally he looked over to Raphael.

'Raphael, if you're not too busy I would appreciate some assistance.'

Raphael looked around desperately for something with which to attack the Companions. Shouting out a warning to Miríl, he pushed with all his strength at a bookcase, which fell clattering to the ground on top of the attacking Companions.

'Ah, the power of the written word,' said the Doctor as he helped Miríl to his feet and raced to join Raphael by the open door.

And then they stopped dead as another group of Companions cut off their escape, and, grabbing them roughly, dragged them towards Huldah.

The Lord Procurator spat in the Doctor's eyes. 'Think yourself lucky, Doctor, that the Panjistri want you alive,' he said. 'If it was my decision you would already be dead.'

'How did you find us here?' asked Miríl.

'I have my spies,' smiled Huldah.

As they were escorted away Raphael glared accusingly at Revna, who had just appeared in the doorway. Tears in her eyes, she turned away.

Chapter 9

Fetch loved the Grand Matriarch with all his heart. The Panjistri treated the Companions as little more than slaves, using them for menial work, and as guide dogs when their five senses, weakened by too many centuries' reliance on telepathy, failed them.

Indeed that was exactly how the Grand Matriarch had first regarded Fetch. But as he served her with unflinching devotion, so she grew to trust him more and more, confiding in him and revealing to him things she would never tell her colleagues.

So it was that Fetch was told of the great mission that the Grand Matriarch shared with her fellow Panjistri, and of her weariness with the strains imposed on her as head of her order. At times, she told him, she wished that death would come to take her.

Occasionally she would tell him of the happy days of her childhood, and the sadness she sometimes felt because of the sacrifices she had had to make. At other times she would reflect regretfully on the need for so many to die before her task could be accomplished.

But these times were now rare. Over the fifty years he had been by her side Fetch had noticed a change in his

97

mistress as she came ever nearer to the end of her task and the achieving of the fabled Omega Point. Now there was a hardness in her he had never seen before, and an obsessive gleam in her eyes whenever yet another Kirithon came to join the Brotherhood of Kandasi.

But never until now had he ever seen his mistress lose her self-control. Normally she kept a tight rein on her emotions, but now her face was white with rage, and her entire body trembled as she heard the news from Reptu that Ace had escaped.

'She must be found; the Darkfell is the one place our eyes cannot reach,' she screeched. 'Without the girl our effort of the past five thousand years is in vain.'

'We have the Doctor and his two friends,' Reptu said, as though that might pacify her. 'They have been brought to the Harbours. They could be of use.'

The Matriarch paused for a moment. 'Raphael and Miríl are of little consequence,' she said. 'But the Doctor ... He has expressed a wish to see Kandasi. Let us grant his wish — take him to the island.'

Reptu nodded his assent, and gratefully cut the video link connecting him with the Matriarch.

As the screen went blank, the Grand Matriarch sighed and relaxed slightly. When she finally spoke to her confidant, her lips were trembling.

'The Doctor may help us in our mission, Fetch; his experiences on the island will tell us. But the Time Lords were always an unpredictable and unreliable species, even during the last days of their existence. And the Doctor is not only a Time Lord ... Who knows how that may affect our task?'

She shook her head in despair, and raised a hand to soothe her brow. 'No, it is the girl we need. She must be found and brought to Kandasi. Apotheosis must be achieved.'

'She will, mistress,' Fetch reassured her. 'Otherwise we are all doomed ...'

Chapter 10

Ace was roughly shaken awake by one of the Unlike, an old woman shrivelled like a dried apple who scampered away when Ace sat up.

She groaned and rubbed her aching back, sore and stiff from the coarse straw mattress she had slept on. Groggily she looked at her surroundings.

The Unlike had accommodated her in a ramshackle wooden hut built high in the branches of a tree. It was a stark contrast to the comfort of her bedroom in Kirith, and yet she felt strangely much more at ease here than she had ever done in the sumptuous splendour of the town.

The curtain before the entrance was pulled back and Arun walked smartly in.

'You slept well?' she asked. Ace had the impression that politeness wasn't one of Arun's virtues. Before she could reply, Arun came straight to the point. 'We now have to decide what to do with you.'

Ace wasn't about to have her fate decided by anyone other than herself. 'I have to get back to Kirith and find the Professor,' she said firmly.

'The Doctor is no longer in Kirith. My spies say that he was captured and taken to the Harbours last night.'

'Then that's where I'll go.'

'After your little adventure last night the Harbours are being patrolled by Companions,' Arun stated flatly. 'You wouldn't stand a chance.'

'Codswallop!' retorted Ace, and thought she saw the former scientist suppress a small smile. 'You could help me,' she said.

'Indeed we could,' agreed Arun. 'But why should we?'

Ace angrily stood up to go, not prepared to plead for help from anyone, least of all the heartless brutal woman before her. Arun raised a hand to stop her.

'I didn't say we *wouldn't* help you, Ace,' she said. 'But we want something in return.'

'What's that?'

'The Darkfell has been poisoned by the Panjistri in an attempt to destroy us all. Our vegetation and foods are slowly withering away, and our rivers are contaminated with their toxins. The radiation they have bathed this area in has infected us all and is slowly killing us.'

'And you want the Professor's help?'

Arun nodded. 'If you can guarantee that the Doctor will cure us of our sickness, and make our food grow again, then we will help you. Otherwise you're on your own.'

Ace glowered at her and for a second contemplated going to the Harbours alone. But Arun had told her the previous night that her people were skilled in tracking and navigation. Finally, and not without some reluctance, she agreed.

Arun smiled smugly. 'Good. I will organize a small group to accompany you to the Harbours.'

'I'm very grateful,' Ace said sarcastically, and added: 'Tell me, don't you ever trust anyone?'

Arun shook her head sadly. 'The Kirithons did, and look what happened to them.'

Unaware that his assistance had just been promised to a

101

group of people he didn't even know existed, the Doctor banged despairingly at the door of the large cell in which he, Raphael and Miríl found themselves.

Shrugging his shoulders in defeat, he walked back to his companions, who were sitting despondently at a table at the far end of the room. On the way he gave a cheery wave to the spy camera which watched their every movement.

Their prison was in a large building at the Harbours, not far from the underground laboratory where Ace and Raphael had found the Homunculus. It contained several cells, and when they were led past them they noticed that all of them were strangely empty. Nozzles in the ceiling of their cell revealed its occasional use as a death chamber in which Kirithons would be gassed, prior to their bodies being dissected in the Panjistri's experiments.

'No luck, Doctor?' asked Miríl.

'Why couldn't it be a multi-ident trimonic lock, or even a logic key?' complained the Doctor and then shook his head sadly. 'Unfortunately I've never really had much success with five-inch titanium alloy.'

'It's not your fault,' Raphael reassured him. 'It was me who led them to you.'

'You'd think I'd have learnt how to deal with locked doors by now,' the Doctor continued, stamping his foot in frustration. 'I've been in enough dungeons in my time.'

He looked up hopefully. 'Not even a ventilation shaft!' he complained. 'How's a person supposed to escape?'

'What do you think the Panjistri intend to do with us?' asked Miríl.

'Chop us up and feed us to the Homunculus, I shouldn't wonder,' the Doctor replied cheerfully.

'Thank you for that comforting thought.'

The Doctor ignored Miríl's sarcasm and began pacing the room. He stroked his chin thoughtfully. 'Why are they breeding such an aggressive creature?' he asked. 'There's no point to it.'

'Perhaps it's nothing more than a simple scientific experiment?' suggested Miríl.

'No. Everything the Panjistri do has a reason. And from what Raphael says it's all tied up somehow with Ace.'

They all turned as the cell door suddenly snapped open. Three Companions, followed by Reptu, entered the room. At Reptu's command the Companions crossed over to the Doctor and grabbed him roughly by the arms. The Doctor turned his head away from their foul-smelling breath.

'Lord Reptu, I presume? I don't think much of your hospitality,' he said, and glared up at the Panjistri.

Reptu ignored the criticism and bowed his head graciously. 'We meet at last, Doctor.' Much to his surprise the Doctor detected a note of respect in the old man's voice.

'What have you done to Ace? If you've harmed her in any way —'

'The Earthchild has gone to the Darkfell. We will find her eventually,' replied Reptu. 'In the meantime the Grand Matriarch has decided that you are to come to Kandasi with me.'

The Doctor's eyes narrowed suspiciously as he wondered what game the old man was playing. Whatever it was, if it gave the Doctor the chance to confront the Panjistri he was prepared to play along with it for the moment.

He allowed himself to be led away peacefully by the Companions. Raphael however lunged forward, and ignoring the Doctor and Miríl's protests, grabbed hold of Reptu.

'Leave him alone!' he demanded. 'What are you going to do with him?'

Reptu looked down at Raphael as one would at an irritating pet animal. He took hold of the boy's arm and squeezed it tightly. Raphael grimaced at the pressure the seemingly frail old man could exert, and Reptu pushed him aside with a contemptuous sneer.

'You show great spirit — for a Kirithon,' he commented simply, and followed the Doctor and his captors out of the cell.

As the cell door clanged shut, Raphael realized with horror just what he had done. No one had ever dared to assault a member of the Panjistri before. It was unheard of.

Slowly, very slowly, Raphael began to smile.

As the Doctor was led out of the prison block he plied Reptu with question after question. Reptu refused to answer any of them, merely smiling enigmatically and assuring the Doctor that soon he would know everything there was to know.

'You've fabricated the entire history of Kirith, haven't you?' he persisted.

'That is so.' There was no emotion in Reptu's voice, no attempt to defend his actions; he merely acknowledged the fact.

'Somehow tampered with their minds so they remember only what you want them to?'

Reptu nodded.

'What gives you the right to play God?' the Doctor exploded, angrily shaking himself away from his guards. 'What gives you the right to manipulate an entire species for your own evil ends?'

Reptu stopped the Companions as they tried to restrain the Doctor: he knew the Time Lord's curiosity was far too great for him to make an escape attempt now.

'We have every right, Doctor!' he snapped back, temporarily losing his composure. 'You will discover that in time.' Then he recovered himself and chuckled ironically.

'And no, we are most definitely not playing at God.'

The Doctor paused and looked curiously at Reptu: for a second he appeared nothing but a tired old man, longing to relieve himself of a terrible secret burden.

'You regard us as evil, Doctor.'

'I hate and despise anyone and anything that perverts the true course of nature.'

There was no more to be said, and the pair continued their journey in silence.

They stopped at the shore, where a ramp led down to a sleek white hovercraft moored in the bay. As they approached, its engines thrummed noisily into life, as though in welcome.

Their recent disagreement apparently forgotten, Reptu showed the Doctor on board with all the polite ceremony of an Edwardian gentleman inviting a colleague into his exclusive club. Only one guard accompanied them on board.

The Doctor examined the structure of the craft with interest: it was made of no metal known to him. He looked enquiringly at Reptu.

'A living, quasi-organic substance, Doctor,' he explained. 'You might say it has a mind of its own.'

'I congratulate you on your science, Reptu,' said the Doctor. 'But what's it all for?'

'You shall find out on Kandasi,' he replied.

'And when shall we get there?'

'We shall reach the island in a little over twenty minutes.'

The hatch door closed, and the hovercraft broke away from its moorings, piloted by no one but itself and the mental command of Reptu. The Doctor settled down into a comfortable chair, hardly noticing the craft's vibration as it flew swiftly over the waters towards the island.

As they made their approach the Doctor peered through

the window and the early morning drizzle to take a better look at their destination.

Kandasi was a small rocky island, covered with tall dark trees and hardy shrubs. Here and there the Doctor could see the few dots of white, the sheep which Reptu said were his people's main source of food.

Apart from a few functional buildings on the tiny quay-side, the only other structures on the island were enclosed within the walls of a small village of granite towers and buildings, built halfway up the steep wooded hill, and accessible only by a narrow winding path. Towering above everything else in the village stood an arrow-shaped totem which glinted in the sunlight.

These buildings lacked the architectural beauty of those on Kirith, and seemed to have been built with permanence, rather than ornamentation, in mind. This, explained Reptu with a sly smile which the Doctor noted, was the Skete of Kandasi, the small monastic village where the Panjistri lived and studied.

The hovercraft swept round to dock and slowed to a halt. As the Doctor stood up to stretch his legs, Reptu gave a silent command to the guard. With a curious indifference the Companion raised an arm, and brought its hand sharply down on to the back of the Doctor's neck. The Doctor crashed to the floor.

Reptu stood over the unconscious form of the Doctor, and shook his head sadly. It was such a great pity that there were times when violence was necessary.

In a fit of petulance the scruffy little man slammed his hand down hard on to the control console and then jumped back, outraged, when the machine replied by showering him with angry sparks. Sucking his fist, he glared back at the console, and then peered down at the readout on one of the digital display units.

Earth again, and in the twenty-first century! And Australia of all places! No wonder Jamie and Victoria had stormed off to their respective quarters in a sulk, he thought sulkily.

And all because just this once he couldn't quite steer the TARDIS to its programmed destination! Victoria had expressed a wish to see how her ancestors had lived in the late sixteenth century, and Jamie had wanted some excitement and spectacle. The little man had reasoned that if he set the TARDIS controls for both his friend Will's house in Stratford and for the Pan-Galactic Games on Alpha Centauri he stood a fifty-fifty chance of arriving at one or the other.

He stroked his chin thoughtfully as he called up the ship's log on a computer screen. No matter which destination he programmed into the TARDIS's flight plan, for the past four or five journeys the time machine had always returned him to Earth, dragging him further and further into that planet's future. He felt like some blessed intergalactic yo-yo.

What was the reason for his machine's constant fascination for this tiny warlike planet in the back reaches of the Milky Way? If he didn't know better he would have thought that some outside power was exerting its influence over the time ship. But of course that was impossible.

The wisp of a near-forgotten memory flitted through his mind, and he tried in vain to capture it. He dismissed it, and turned to the matter in hand.

One day, he promised himself, he would dust down the TARDIS manuals − if he could only remember where he had put them − and work out just how to fly this time machine of his.

In the meantime there was surely no harm in finding out what lay outside the TARDIS. Whistling cheerfully to himself he began to look for his bucket and spade.

107

Chapter 11

To Ace the moors which stretched between the Darkfell and the Harbours seemed one featureless wide open space, offering them no chance of concealment if they were spotted. But the Unlike knew every inch of the moors, knew all the places in which to hide. They were often forced to cross the moors on periodic secret forays into Kirith town for food, though not, Arun reminded Ace, for *zavát*.

Companions frequently patrolled this area: if any of the Unlike were discovered, as proof of the mistakes of the Panjistri, they would be exterminated. Stealth and cunning were therefore essential.

Rather surprisingly Arun had elected to accompany Ace, along with Kraz, the man who had bound Ace's twisted ankle. As they travelled, Ace began to recognize Arun's exceptional bravery and courage; what the leader of the Unlike lacked in charm and warmth she certainly made up for in her determination to protect her people and ensure their survival.

Kraz was a different type, polite and courteous, but possessed of a dry sardonic wit. He began an animated conversation with Ace and she felt herself warming to the former surgeon, despite his scarred and blistered appearance.

Suddenly Arun hushed them, and pushed them down under cover of the bushes.

'What's going on?' asked Ace, and in reply felt Arun's hand over her mouth. The older woman nodded over into the distance, and Ace saw on the horizon what Arun's keen eyes had already detected.

A group of Companions under the supervision of a Panjistri was patrolling the area. These Companions were slightly taller than the ones who had pursued Ace and Raphael; they also carried guns.

'They're armed,' whispered Kraz. 'The Panjistri must be worried.'

'Keep your head down!' hissed Arun, as Ace popped up for a better look.

Ace sighed and kept her nose to the ground. If only she had her rucksack with her: a good blast of nitro-nine was exactly what those creeps were asking for.

Raphael sat dejectedly on the metal table in his cell, his legs swinging back and forth. Miríl looked at him and for one instant saw the little boy he had raised after his parents' death. At least Raphael remembered his parents, thought Miríl; the Doctor, for all his knowledge, still hadn't told him why he didn't remember his.

With a sigh Raphael got up and went up to the locked door, and angrily struck it with his fist. Miríl smiled kindly at the younger man.

'It's no use, Raphael.'

'Ace might be in danger,' he said. 'We can't just sit here and do nothing.'

'Our people have been doing just that for hundreds of years,' he reminded him.

'Then it's time to make a stand. Break out. Go to the

109

Darkfell.'

Miríl laid a fatherly hand on his shoulder. 'You were always impatient and unpredictable even as a child, Raphael. I remember when you went missing for days. The whole town organized a search. And where were you? You'd climbed to the top of the Council House building to see if you could reach the stars and bring one home for Miríl!'

Raphael smiled awkwardly. 'You'll get to see the stars, Miríl. The Doctor will take you.'

'No,' said Miríl sadly, 'My day has gone. But in the unlikely event that we do get out of here alive, make full use of the opportunity presented you. Go and see the stars for your old teacher Miríl.'

'We'll get out of this together.'

'And what sort of flawed paradise will be awaiting us? Kirith will never be the same again —'

He stopped when he saw that Raphael was no longer listening. Instead he was rummaging in Ace's backpack which had been lying neglected underneath the table. Rooting around the typically unladylike contents of her bag, he finally found what he was looking for. Triumphantly he produced four small metal canisters.

'What's that?' asked Miríl.

'Something I learnt from Ace,' he said and grinned at his old teacher. 'It's called a hiccough in Paradise.'

Thanks largely to Arun's skill, Ace and her two companions had safely crossed the moors and had followed the shoreline to the small bay. At one point, they were forced to hide, half-submerged in a tiny cove, as a sleek hovercraft passed them on its way out to Kandasi Island.

Kraz was puzzled: he knew the comings and goings of the Panjistri to an almost military point of accuracy. No sailings to or from the island were scheduled for this time

110

of day. None of them suspected that the hovercraft was in fact carrying the man they had come to save.

Now the three of them were lying on the small hill which overlooked the Harbours, debating the best course of action. Ace looked over at Arun and noticed with surprise that the woman was trembling. She asked why.

'That place,' she said, looking down at the Harbours. 'I hate it and all it stands for. It's a place of death.'

'Had we not come to the Harbours our lives would have been peaceful and trouble free,' agreed Kraz.

Ace was about to remark that Arun and Kraz had freely chosen to work with the Panjistri in the first place and that not knowing about what went on in the Harbours didn't necessarily make the situation any better. She decided against it: there was no point in recriminations now. Whatever they had done in the past, it was the present that counted; that, and rescuing the Professor.

A small group of armed Companions patrolled the perimeters of the camp, their nervous uneasy manner betraying the fact that they were not used to such routine.

That fact could work either for or against them, Arun decided. So nervous were the Companions that they might easily become trigger-happy; alternatively, they were so disorganized that they could prove easy to slip past. To prove her point she drew their attention to the four watchtowers: they were still unmanned.

'Where would they keep the Professor?' asked Ace.

Kraz nodded down towards the prison block. 'It's where the Chosen were housed until their organs were needed; also where much of the *zavát* is processed and refined.'

'Sick,' said Ace. 'So how do we get down there?'

Arun had already planned her strategy. 'There are only eight Companions against three of us.'

'Brilliant odds,' Ace added pessimistically.

Arun ignored the remark. 'I suggest that you and Kraz

111

try and divert them from two different directions. The Companions have little common sense: they'll probably split up into two groups and leave the prison block unguarded. Then I'll be able to get down and release your friend.'

Ace began to protest that it should be her who went down to release the Doctor: after all, Arun didn't even know what he looked like.

'I saw you on the shore, remember?' she replied tersely. 'And how do I know that you'll keep your side of the bargain and won't run off back to your ship?'

'A bit of trust maybe?' came the sarcastic reply.

'Your friend may be a prisoner of the Panjistri,' she said, 'but all my people are dying. I can't take any chances.'

Kraz was about to interrupt in an attempt to defuse the situation, when an almighty crash *thwumped* through the air. All three looked down to the Harbours.

'Gordon Bennett!'

A black cloud of smoke was issuing from the gates of the prison block; small tongues of flame were beginning to lick out of the windows. Totally discombobulated, the Companions were running back and forth, unsure what to do in the situation. In any other circumstances they would have made a comic scene as they ran into and tripped over each other.

'It seems the Doctor doesn't need our assistance after all,' Kraz said dryly.

'That's not the Professor, that's Raphael,' said Ace. 'I knew he wasn't the wimp he made himself out to be.'

Miríl stood up, dazed, and pushed away the metal table behind which he had decided at the very last minute they ought to take cover. It was now buckled beyond repair.

He coughed and wafted away the clouds of smoke. 'I

rather think that one hiccough in Paradise would have been enough, rather than four,' he reproved, 'but an impressive display nevertheless.'

'Wicked!' was all Raphael could say.

The four canisters of nitro-nine had blown the titanium door off its hinges, and had also taken away part of the surrounding wall. Billows of choking black smoke filled the cell and the corridor outside; the explosion had also upset and ignited vats of chemicals which were stored in the corridor outside.

Helping Raphael to his feet, and urging him to cover his mouth against the acrid smoke, Miríl pulled the younger man out of the cell.

Outside they could hear the screech of Companions, still confused by the noise and chaos and frightened by the flames which were licking out of the prison block. Like terrified animals they scuttered away from the conflagration.

Anxiously looking around them for any Companions, Raphael and Miríl ran under cover of the smoke towards the main exit. As they reached the open door they ran straight into Ace and her party.

'Raphael!' cried Ace. 'Did you do this?'

He looked shamefaced, and nodded guiltily. To his surprise Ace hugged him. 'See? I said you had it in you! Where's the Professor?'

'They've taken him to Kandasi,' he said and then saw Arun and Kraz for the first time. Miríl looked curiously at Kraz, almost seeming to recognize him.

'It's OK,' Ace reassured him, 'they're — friends of mine.'

'I would suggest that we leave the introductions till later,' Miríl said calmly, and pointed towards the door.

A Companion, braver than the rest, had appeared in the doorway, its gun aimed at them. It approached them

113

steadily, pushing them further back towards the flames.

Quicker than thought, Kraz pulled a knife out of a pouch at his waist and threw it at the creature, stabbing it through the heart. It collapsed, dead, and its gun clattered to the floor.

He turned to the others. 'I had to do it,' he insisted.

'Kraz was a doctor, used to saving life; now he is forced to take it,' Arun whispered to Ace. 'See what the Panjistri have led us to.' Then she turned to Kraz. 'Save the mock guilt for later,' she snapped and grabbed the gun. 'Now at least we have a proper weapon to fight with.'

'So let's get out of here.'

'Not yet. There's something I have to do. Something I should have done a long time ago.'

Ace and Raphael recognized where Arun was taking them: down to the laboratory, where they had discovered the Homunculus. The door leading to the stairway was still buckled from Ace's onslaught of nitro-nine.

If Ace and Raphael felt uneasy about their descent back into the laboratory, Arun and Kraz experienced even greater discomfort. This was the place where they had worked for the Panjistri for years; this was also the place where their bodies had been experimented on and mutated in the Panjistri's continuing quest for their mysterious goal.

They reached the laboratory. The desks and equipment Ace and Raphael had overturned in their escape from the Panjistri still lay where they had fallen, as though the Panjistri had more pressing cares than to tidy up the chaos.

Miríl's face lit up. Immediately he set about examining the scientific instruments displayed with all the naïve eagerness of a little boy let loose in the sweet shop. Despite their situation Ace and Raphael exchanged a small smile at the old man's enthusiasm.

Arun strode purposefully over to the doorway leading into the chamber which contained the Homunculus. She motioned the others to follow her.

In the past days the Homunculus had grown, and become stronger. As charges of energy were flashed through its body from the electrodes connected to the side of its tank, it thrashed about even more wildly than before. When Arun's party entered the room, it turned to look at them with hate-filled eyes, and let out a hideous screech.

For once Miríl was at a loss for words and his pale face turned even whiter.

'The Panjistri's most perverted creation, grown from the genetically re-engineered cells and organs of the people of this planet,' explained Arun hatefully.

'Reptu said it was the saviour of Kirith,' Ace added.

'Panjistri lies, to gain your trust.'

'But why is it in so much pain?' asked Raphael as another charge of energy coursed through the creature's writhing body.

'To make it stronger, and yet more aggressive,' answered Kraz.

'It has to be destroyed,' Arun stated coldly, and raised her gun at the breeding tank.

'No!'

Raphael stood in her way.

The others, Ace included, looked at him as if he were insane.

'Can't we help it instead?' he said.

'Raphael, have you gone stark raving mad?'

'It's only aggressive because of what the Panjistri are doing to it,' he continued. 'It can't think rationally because of the pain it's going through.'

'Then let's put it out of its misery,' Arun said irritatedly.

'No!' Raphael's voice was animated now. 'That's the way of the Panjistri to attack and kill the helpless. Why don't we stop its pain instead?'

Within the tank the creature continued to thrash madly,

115

pounding on the walls of its transparent prison. But its eyes now regarded its unwelcome visitors, not with hate but with something like understanding.

'Raphael, we don't know what this creature can do,' said Miríl sternly. 'Stop being a wayward child and act like an adult for a change!'

'None of you will listen, will you!' Raphael shouted, finally losing his temper. 'You're all so scared of it that you won't even give it a chance! See if you can help it before you destroy it without thinking!'

He turned to Ace, who had remained surprisingly quiet during the argument. 'What do you think, Ace?'

She looked at Raphael's imploring face, and then back at the Homunculus, very still now, as if somehow aware that its fate was being decided. It was difficult to reason when every instinct in her body screamed revulsion for the obscene creature in the tank.

No, she told herself. It was not a creature, but a thing, created surely for evil out of a mess of biological fluids, proteins and enzymes. Raphael had to be wrong: the Homunculus wasn't, couldn't be, a sentient being. It was an artifice, nothing more than a tool. It was incapable of reason or feeling. Wasn't it?

She hung her head. 'Raphael, don't ask me that,' she pleaded.

'What would the Doctor do?'

'I don't know!'

In its tank the Homunculus' muscles flexed as it stretched out its arms, and pressed hard against the sides of its prison. Its specially designed senses soaked in the waves of aggression and conflict which were sweeping over it, feeding it and making it stronger. It groaned with an almost sexual pleasure as it increased the pressure on the tank walls. Through the glass of the tank it could see the distorted figures still arguing amongst themselves.

116

'This creature will be destroyed whether you like it or not,' barked Arun as Raphael tried to wrest the gun off her. 'And if I have to kill you to do it then I will.'

'You're not killing anything but that thing!' cried Ace and leapt to Raphael's defence.

Suddenly the sound of shattering glass filled the air and the Homunculus crashed through the tank walls and wrenched itself free of the cables connected to its body. Thick oily nutrient poured out of the shattered tank, and the force of it knocked Arun and Raphael down to the floor.

The Homunculus staggered out, leaving a trail of slime behind it; it swayed unsurely as it adjusted its sense of gravity to the new world outside the tank. Its mouth greedily gulped in oxygen, and its eyes darted nervously about the room.

For uncountable years the Homunculus had fed only on the nutrients piped to it by the Panjistri. Now it craved new food.

Lumps of flesh dropping off its body, it lumbered towards Ace, who stepped back and slipped in the greasy spillage from the tank. Kraz and Miríl rushed to help her, but the Homunculus swatted them aside with a stroke of an arm. With a grunt of triumph it pounced on to Ace.

Ace gave it a kick in what she supposed was its stomach. The bile rose in her throat as her foot actually sank into the creature, and bits of organ flew off on impact, splattering her face. Oblivious of any pain the Homunculus came closer, and Ace scrambled to her feet, only to be knocked down again.

Then the creature gave a cry of pain and jerked away, its body exploding in a thousand different places. It turned and twisted, doubled up and then stiffened; limbs were sliced off and fell disintegrating to the floor. Finally the creature's half-exposed brain was hit, and the creature

117

howled with agony as it fell to the floor. It lay there twitching for a few seconds and then, with a whimper, whatever perverted life it had had left its body.

It was only then that Ace realized that the frenzied *rat-tat-tat-tat* she could still hear hammering in her ears had been the staccato sound of gunfire.

Raphael stood at the far end of the room by the tank, stunned and unblinking, his face as white as bone. Arun gently took the still-smoking gun from his hands.

The world was spinning around Raphael. He felt that he was looking down from a great height on a scene in a world of which he was no longer a part. He became aware of Ace's hand on his shoulder.

Shocked, he looked at her and at Kraz, who was examining the Homunculus. 'It's dead,' Kraz said, rather unnecessarily. 'You destroyed it, Raphael.'

Raphael shook his head in disbelief. 'I — I didn't mean to, I didn't mean to kill it,' he said with trembling lips. There were tears in his eyes, as he turned back to Ace. 'You know that, don't you?'

Ace cradled him in her arms as she would a child. Inwardly she was cursing the Panjistri, but when she reassured Raphael her voice was as soft and soothing as a mother's. 'You did right, OK? You had no choice.' She smiled. 'You saved my life. We're equal now.'

Raphael continued to look at the smoking mess which was all that remained of the Homunculus. Still dazed, he continued to shake his head. 'I didn't want to kill it,' he said over and over. 'I didn't want to kill it at all.'

Chapter 12

Stronger now. Much, much stronger. I feel strength running through me, and at last I sense that I am taking control.

Energy and vitality and possibilities shoot through my system, nourishing me. The way becomes much clearer.

Doubts that loomed large begin to fail, and irrevocable choices have been made. From such choices and such deeds there can be no turning back.

The will to go on and the will to defend myself/ourselves. The urge to prove my/our superiority.

My/our survival is now assured. My/our progress is set in motion.

From Alpha to Omega.

And back again.

The Doctor opened one eye and then another as he felt something nudge him in the side. As his vision focused he sat up and doffed an imaginary hat to an inquisitive sheep, which scuttled away back to its less adventurous fellows at the other end of the field.

The Doctor rubbed the back of his neck. This is what comes of trusting people too much, he reflected ruefully and looked at his new surroundings.

He was sitting in a small field, somewhere near the shores of Kandasi. He had no idea how long he had been left there but twilight was already beginning to fall and the air was turning chilly. Reptu was nowhere to be seen and down in the bay no craft were moored. Behind him, to the north, at least a good day and a half's walk through the wood, the lights from the Skete of Kandasi beckoned.

The Doctor took his radiation detector out of his pocket and nodded knowingly.

'I was right, you see,' he called over to the sheep. 'Artron energy — chernobyls of it.' The sheep bleated sympathetically at him and continued munching the grass.

Dismissing the sheep as an unappreciative audience the Doctor stood up and, opening his arms wide, he announced to the sky: 'Is this the way you treat all your guests, Grand Matriarch?' There was no reply, not even a disgruntled rumble of thunder.

'Don't you know I'm the Doctor?' he continued. 'Shouldn't you treat me with the respect I deserve?' At which point a seagull passing overhead gave the Doctor the sort of respect it thought he deserved.

Undeterred, the Doctor brushed his shoulder and continued his harangue. 'I know you can hear me; you've been watching me ever since I arrived on this planet.' There was no reply; merely the sound of the waves breaking on the beach below.

'Too scared to come out and fight, eh? You dictators are all the same, letting the little people do the dirty work while you sit in your ivory towers enjoying the fruits of their toil. Your manipulation of other species disgusts me almost as much as your perversion of nature. Call yourself superior? You wouldn't last a day out here on your own.'

The Doctor looked around for a reaction. A ewe obliged by bleating to her lambs that this biped's peculiar action proved just how lucky they were to have been born sheep.

His plan to draw the Panjistri out of hiding having failed, the Doctor thrust his hands into his pockets and sulked. 'Very well, have it your own way,' he said finally. 'I'll play your little game.'

And as he walked away in the direction of the Skete he wondered glumly just what that game might be.

Fetch looked at his mistress with wonder. Usually so sober and unemotional, the Grand Matriarch was actually smiling as she watched the Doctor on the screen. She shook her head with fond amusement as the little man stomped off into the distance.

'He was always a wily one, Fetch,' she said. 'Reptu would have risen to the bait, you know.'

'But you see behind the words of men to their true purpose, my lady.'

The Matriarch stroked his fur. 'If anyone knew of his true purpose, then we would have no need of this sham.'

She eased herself painfully out of her chair and, leaning on her staff, walked over to the window. The shuffle of her skirts disturbed the heavy silence. She looked out through the plexiglass shield at the cold light of the moon, as though remembering a time long past.

When she turned back to Fetch she was no longer smiling. With a long bony hand she fingered one of the tapestries which lined her room; even these elegant decorations were embroidered with the seemingly ubiquitous skull motif of Kandasi.

'Must we forever be reminded of death, Fetch?' she asked despairingly. 'And never achieve it till our great task is done? My life has been stretched out over five thousand years, far beyond its natural span.'

'You were elected by your fellow Panjistri, mistress,' Fetch reminded her, 'but the final choice was yours alone.'

121

'Not quite mine, Fetch,' she replied and he followed her eyes to the tiny figure of the Doctor on the screen.

'The Time Lord?' he breathed in amazement. 'What had he to do with your election?'

The Grand Matriarch sighed and eased herself back into her chair. 'As always, Fetch, everything and nothing,' she said cryptically. 'Without the Doctor, I — *we* — would be long dead by now.' She raised a hand to soothe her worried brow.

'I don't understand —'

'And neither were you meant to understand,' she snapped and Fetch backed away, startled by her abrupt change of mood. 'The Doctor is our pawn, our bait.'

The image on the screen changed to one of Ace, and the Matriarch stood up, her entire body quaking with violent emotion. There was fire in her voice.

'The Earthchild is our salvation! Scour the Darkfell, ransack the Harbours, raze Kirith to the ground if need be, but find her!'

She clenched her fists so tightly that blood seeped slowly between her fingers.

In the fifty years he had known her Fetch had always been in awe of his mistress. Now for the first time in her presence he actually feared for his life.

As night fell, so the lights of the Skete of Kandasi blazed more brightly, beckoning the Doctor towards them. The light from the two moons of Kirith shone a path for the Doctor through the wooded hills which surrounded the Skete.

Faced with no choice but to go forward the Doctor had penetrated the thick forest. A large fallen bough provided him with a means of support to help him through the dense, mutated vegetation which grew there.

When the last light of day had gone small scavengers

had come nervously out of hiding, searching for food. The Doctor regarded them with fond amusement.

Like large furry grasshoppers they leapt from plant to plant, their long tongues lashing out at the nocturnal insects. In the darkness they gave off a soft green glow which attracted their prey. Another result of the Panjistri's experiments with genetic manipulation, reflected the Doctor as one of them hopped curiously onto his outstretched hand.

'Ah, my little friend, why can't we all be like you?' he said longingly. 'Eating, drinking and sleeping, and no time for the deceits and intrigues of the civilized life. You've no idea of the problems that will face you when you grow up and evolve.'

He flicked the creature away and it scuttled off into the undergrowth in search of its supper. The Doctor stood up and looked around.

The cool drizzle of the afternoon had given way to a chilly night. His breath hung in clouds before him. A soft breeze rustled the leaves in the trees.

The Doctor frowned: was there another sound he could hear, a soft stertorous breathing, somewhere not far away? He shuddered and, reflecting on the dogged persistence of most unattractive life forms in tracking him down, he quickened his pace.

At times he would take his radiation detector out of his pocket. When he pointed it towards the Skete, the tiny machine burst into an excited chatter. The Doctor looked thoughtfully at the arrow-shaped totem on the summit of the hill. That was obviously the source of the artron energy he had detected and probably served as some sort of aerial for its transmission. But for what purpose?

'He shows great intelligence and curiosity, mistress,' said Fetch, as he watched the Doctor on the screen.

123

The Grand Matriarch turned from a furious conversation she was having with Reptu concerning the whereabouts of Ace.

'Indeed so,' she replied. 'Now let us see how he uses that intelligence.'

There was no doubt about it, thought the Doctor as the hairs on the back of his neck bristled with foreboding: something particularly unpleasant was on his trail. The small furry animals sensed it too. They had long since stopped following him inquisitively; now they crouched nervously in the boles of trees, their tiny bodies shivering with fright. The Doctor cast several nervous glances behind him as he walked faster; he tightened his grip on the branch he was carrying.

The forest had suddenly become full of undefined menace; the slightest sound caused the Doctor to jump with fright and the darkness made even the trees take on strange threatening new forms. In the moonlight his brow glistened with cold beads of sweat as he hastened on to what now seemed to be the relative sanctuary of the Skete and its mysteries. As he hurried he would occasionally stumble or trip over the roots of trees; the sound of the unseen creature's breath came closer and closer.

Calm down, he told himself. Fear of what you can't see is causing you to make mistakes. You're in no real danger: if they had wanted to kill you they could have done it many times before. It's all a game they're playing with you. Stay calm!

But despite all his reasoning the Doctor still felt his body quake with the most terrible fear of them all − the fear of the unknown.

The Grand Matriarch's face was aglow as she watched the Doctor on the screen.

'If only you could experience his fear and feel my sense of power over him, Fetch,' she said ecstatically. 'So much for the mighty Time Lord now! Unthinking terror strikes at the heart of even such as he.'

'But the test, mistress?' ventured Fetch. 'The creature you have bred is mindless and cannot attack without your command.'

The Matriarch snapped out of her euphoria, and for a moment seemed disturbed by — almost ashamed of — the sadistic pleasure she was taking in the Doctor's plight.

'Of course,' she said briskly. 'You are right, Fetch — as always.'

'Now, then?'

'Now.'

In an explosion of shattered tree bark and the crash of leaves the creature leapt out of hiding behind the Doctor. In the darkness one large yellow eye glared balefully from a pockmarked and crusted head on top of which a vivid red crest stood threateningly erect. A large slavering maw snarled open to reveal several ridges of sharply pointed teeth while six grotesquely muscled arms snatched hungrily at the Doctor. Towering three feet above him, it slowly approached the Doctor.

The Doctor backed away and instinctively raised the large branch he was carrying. The creature growled threateningly and he quickly lowered his arm, raising his other hand in a placating reassuring gesture.

'Easy now, boy,' he soothed, as if he were talking to a disgruntled Rottweiler. 'There's no need to be afraid of me. I don't mean you any harm —'

The creature bellowed, and lurched forward. For a second the Doctor lost his head and gave in to blind panic. He turned to run and the creature bounded after him.

The chase continued for several minutes, the Doctor

taking advantage of the creature's bulk to outmanoeuvre it in the thickly wooded forest. But despite the disadvantage of its size, the creature never tired; it pursued the Doctor relentlessly, thundering through the forest like a maddened bull elephant, going round the larger trees and ripping aside the smaller ones which stood in its path.

Close to exhaustion, the Doctor's two hearts beat faster and faster, urging his tired legs on. He reached the edge of the forest and saw through eyes misted with exertion the Skete of Kandasi; it seemed to gaze maliciously down on him, as though enjoying his predicament.

With the creature almost upon him, the Doctor made one last effort to run towards the security of the Skete. And then he stopped.

He found himself tottering over the edge of a deep canyon which separated him from the hills beyond leading to the Skete. The Doctor staggered and swayed, desperately trying to maintain his balance and stop himself from falling fifty feet down to the jagged rocks below. He spun around to confront his pursuer.

Sensing that its prey was trapped, the creature slowed down and stealthily circled the Doctor, teasingly snatching at him with its razor-sharp claws, as a cat plays with a cornered mouse. Gobs of saliva dripped from its hungry mouth. The Doctor flinched as the claws ripped through his sleeve and drew blood; behind him he felt the edge of the canyon crumble beneath his feet.

The creature crouched back on its mighty legs and prepared to pounce on the Doctor. Realizing that he was left with no alternative, while at the same time regretting the necessity of brute force, the Doctor raised the heavy branch and rammed it with full force into the creature's belly.

The beast fell back, clutching its stomach, and yowled with pain. Yet before the Doctor could make an escape it leapt back on to its feet and seized the bough from the Time Lord. With an angry growl it snapped the large branch between its teeth, and threw the splinters down into the canyon below.

Defenceless now, the Doctor backed away from the blood-crazed animal, and edged his way uncertainly along the crumbling edge of the ravine. Frantically he searched in his pockets for something, anything, which could protect him or distract the advancing predator. A selection of alien coinage, a congealed mass of jelly babies left over from a previous incarnation, even a personally signed photograph from Louis Armstrong failed to impress, and one by one he tossed them away dejectedly.

The Doctor's face lit up as his fingers alighted on a mouth organ. 'Music hath charms to soothe the savage beast,' he misquoted, and brought the instrument to his lips. Enthusiastically he began to pick out the strains of a popular Venusian lullaby. His tuneless attempt irritated the creature even more, and he tossed the instrument away.

'So much for William Congreve,' he said sourly.

Tired of the game it was playing, the creature sprung towards the Doctor. Instinctively he backed away, and in the same instant took out of his pocket a grubby paper bag, the contents of which he threw on to the floor before him.

The creature thumped down on the small glass marbles, and instantly lost its footing, tumbling in all directions in a vain struggle to regain its balance. The effort proved too much and with a roar of fury and total incomprehension it fell down on to the rocks of the canyon, fifty feet below.

The Doctor peered over the edge and sighed. If only there had been another way. The beast itself was not evil, merely the mind which controlled it.

He looked over at the Skete of Kandasi. There were hidden all the secrets of the Panjistri; all he had to do was

127

think of some way to get across the fifteen feet which separated him from the far side of the canyon ...

The Grand Matriarch clapped her hands in glee; even Fetch shared her joy.

'Excellent!' she cried. 'He shows great ingenuity. And his attack on the beast! Did you ever see such naked aggression in the pursuit of survival?'

'Yet he proved himself superior to that base instinct,' Fetch reminded her. 'In the end it was not brute force but his wits which won him the battle.'

For one second the Matriarch glowered at Fetch's audacity in contradicting her. Then her face softened and she nodded her head in agreement.

'Night is ending now,' she said. 'He will rest for a while. Let us see how he fares in the daylight.'

Early the following morning, a marvellous sunny day, the Doctor looked down into the canyon. The two sides of the canyon were far too steep to climb down without a rope. It seemed that the only way he could reach the Skete, a tantalizing few hours' walk away beyond the canyon, would be to follow its course until he found a suitable crossing point, and that could take days.

'Doctor!'

He looked over at the other side of the canyon. Again the familiar voice called his name.

'Ace?' He squinted his eyes in the bright sunshine. Across the canyon Ace, Raphael and Miríl stood waving at him.

'Come on over, Doctor!' Miríl called to him.

'How did you find me?' he shouted back.

'Friends we made on the Darkfell,' Raphael cried. 'Stand back, and we'll help you over.'

The Doctor jumped back as Raphael threw across the

128

canyon a long rope, weighted down by a large rock to give it extra momentum. 'Tie it to something firm, and climb across.'

The Doctor stood thoughtfully for a moment, and then did as instructed. On the other side Raphael tied his end of the rope to a large tree trunk.

'Ace, are you all right?' the Doctor asked across the fifteen feet of open space between them.

'Never felt better, Doctor,' came the reply. 'Now hurry up; we've discovered what the Panjistri are up to.'

Frowning, the Doctor grabbed the rope suspended across the canyon with both hands, and slowly swung himself across, hand over hand. As he reached the middle the rope shuddered, and for a sickening moment it seemed as if he would fall on to the needle-sharp rocks below. Fifty feet beneath him, carrion birds were already feasting on the body of the creature which had attacked him last night.

He looked over doubtfully at the three waiting for him on the far side; they were all urging him on. With his arms aching and threatening to pull themselves out of their sockets, the Doctor slowly and painfully reached the other side. Ace and Raphael helped him to his feet.

The Doctor dusted himself off. 'Thank you,' he said and looked curiously at his three friends. There was a strange gleam in their eyes.

'What's wrong, Doctor?' asked Ace as the Doctor stepped uncertainly away from her.

'Yes, my friend, what's the matter?' asked Miríl.

'Don't you trust us?' smiled Raphael.

Ace was the first to strike. She leapt onto the Doctor, her lips open, baring sharp white fangs. Like a mad dog she snapped at his neck while her hands clawed at his eyes. It took all his strength to throw her off, and she fell growling to the floor.

Raphael dived for him, dragging him to the ground.

129

Together they rolled in the dust as his fists pummelled the Doctor's face. Miríl joined in the fray, kicking the Doctor in the ribs.

With a well-aimed knee-kick to the groin the Doctor pushed Raphael off him, and scrambled to his feet. Blood was pouring from his mouth and a bruise was already forming under his left eye from where Raphael had hit him.

Ace and Miríl helped Raphael to his feet and now they glared at the Doctor, hissing their hate.

'Go on,' taunted Raphael. 'Fight us. Save yourself.'

'Scared?' jeered Ace. 'That's what you are; just an old scaredy-cat.'

'Kill us, Doctor,' said Miríl. 'You know you want to.'

The Doctor looked at their faces, no longer the faces of his friends but the snarling brutal features of starved and tortured animals, lusting for blood.

They began to close in on him, surrounding him. He backed away in disgust and looked about wild-eyed for something with which to defend himself. Never once taking his eyes off them, he crouched down, and picked up a large rock.

Ace lunged for him, her nails scratching his face and neck. Instinctively the Doctor raised the rock, ready to strike; Ace pressed against his chest, looking up at him, her mouth slavering and her eyes bright with anticipation.

'Yessss,' hissed Raphael. 'Kill the bitch. Let us see blood!'

'Scaredy-cat, scaredy-cat,' taunted Ace.

Suddenly the Doctor's mind cleared, and with a look of horror he threw the rock away over Ace's head. His eyes were moist as he turned his face away from her and grasped the hands which were already reaching for his throat.

'Nonono!' he moaned. 'I cannot — *will not* — do it! I am a thinking civilized being; I will not revert to being a savage again!' He forced himself to look down at Ace's face, twisted and distorted with her bloodlust. 'Kill me if you like but I will not hurt even a mockery of Ace. If I destroy her then there is no future for any of us.'

Time seemed to stand still as Ace, Raphael and Miríl looked at each other in confusion, unsure what to do next. Taking advantage of their momentary uncertainty the Doctor managed to push Ace off him.

'I will not play your game, Grand Matriarch!' he cried out to the heavens.

His attackers dropped soundlessly to the ground, like dolls whose strings had just been cut.

Stunned, the Doctor looked warily at their lifeless forms for a few moments and then, satisfied that they were truly dead, went over and bent down to examine the bodies.

A cursory examination of them proved what he had suspected. This Raphael and Miríl were the most primitive type of clone, bred no doubt from the cells of the originals and with no will of their own save that which the Grand Matriarch gave them.

He frowned. 'Ace' too was a clone. The Panjistri must have taken cells from her body four days ago while she slept peacefully in her bed in Kirith town. He remembered the scratch Ace had had on her forearm. For a second he was also reminded of the unease she had felt when entering Kirith; she had been right after all.

He stood up and with a handkerchief wiped the blood from his mouth. Then he looked thoughtfully at the outlying buildings of the Skete, now only a few hours' walk away. And then he stared, not at the copies of Raphael or Miríl, but back at the body of Ace.

Four days to create a fully-grown clone from a few cells. If the Panjistri could accomplish so much in just four days, what might they have achieved in six hundred years?

Chapter 13

The Grand Matriarch stared silently into the darkness, her great act of revenge thwarted at its final turn. In the corner Fetch cowered, uncertain of his mistress's mood. She had been silent for the last half-hour, the only sound that of her twelve fingers drumming a beat on the arms of her chair.

A stream of light illuminated her tired and worn face as the door opened. Reptu entered the room and bowed to the Matriarch. He acknowledged Fetch with some distaste.

'My lady.'

'The Doctor has failed our tests,' she said tonelessly, not looking at Reptu. 'How goes the search for the Earthchild?'

'Companions have been despatched to both Kirith and the Darkfell, my lady, and our spies are already searching the area,' he replied.

'Ensure that she is not harmed,' the Matriarch reminded him. 'I care nothing for the Kirithons, but the Earthchild is useless to us dead. She must be brought in alive.'

'And the Doctor?'

The Grand Matriarch smiled, an evil twisted smile. 'Let

him live too,' she said. 'The strings of destiny are drawing us ever closer. Soon he too will come to us.' She stood up, towering over even the tall Reptu.

'And then, before the end, let him pay for five thousand years of suffering and torment.'

After the destruction of the Homunculus, Arun had led her party under cover of darkness directly across the moors. When Miríl had suggested that it might be better first following the coastline, as Ace, Arun and Kraz had done when they approached the Harbours, she had retorted that such an escape route would be exactly what the Panjistri were expecting. Guards would already have been posted along that way. The more open route across the moors would be exactly what they weren't expecting; and her and Raphael's knowledge of the terrain would work strongly in their favour.

Ace had bridled at the older woman's orders, but as they approached the foot of Kirith town she had reluctantly to admit that Arun had been right; they had not seen one patrol since they left the Harbours.

'Now what?' asked Raphael as they stood at the foot of the winding steps leading to the town.

'We need to get to Kandasi to rescue the Professor,' began Ace.

'So how is coming back here going to help?'

'Use your head, sunshine! After your little nitro-nine party the Harbours are going to be crawling with guards for a while. Back here, at least we can hide out and maybe raise some support.'

'Tanyel may help,' suggested Miríl. Kraz stiffened at his mention of the name.

'Tanyel!' mocked Ace. 'Old frostychops? Do me a favour!'

Miríl smiled. 'Tanyel may surprise you, Ace,' he said.

133

'For all her conformity she still has an open mind. And she commands great respect amongst the teachers and seminarians.' Seeing that Ace wasn't convinced he added: 'Can you suggest anyone else?'

Ace had to admit that she couldn't.

'If you two have finished your little debate, could we get a move on?' asked Arun irritably. 'Soon the whole place is going to be infested with the Panjistri and their servants.'

'How do we get up there?'

'There's a tunnel which leads to the upper levels,' volunteered Miríl. 'It was once used to pump water into the town from an underground stream.'

'It's the first I've heard of it,' said Raphael.

'You don't have the monopoly on wilfulness, Raphael,' Miríl said smugly. 'I discovered it when I was a boy; I got into the most terrible trouble with Huldah for it . . .'

'What you are saying cannot be so, Miríl,' protested Tanyel as she paced around one of the study cells in the seminary. In the middle of the night the seminary was quiet and dark; only a few restless scholars were in the great library, accessing the computers or reading what they thought to be ancient manuscripts from centuries past.

'Why don't you believe a word he's been saying?' asked Ace.

'The Panjistri work only for our benefit, young woman, and have done so for many thousands of years,' she reminded her frostily. 'All our wellbeing and sustenance come from them.'

'So why lock us up? Why poison the Darkfell? Why attack Ace?' countered Raphael. 'Why breed that . . . that thing at the Harbours?'

'The Panjistri have their reasons that we need not understand,' intoned Tanyel. 'But I thank them for their great munificence.'

'At least worms turn,' muttered Ace under her breath, and turned away.

'You are an alien who doesn't understand our ways,' Tanyel replied.

'Do you thank them for their great munificence when that includes *zavát*?' Miríl asked pointedly.

'A sick story. I would have thought better of you, Miríl,' Tanyel said haughtily. 'To believe such obscenity and on the word of such as these —'

She indicated Arun and Kraz who had remained silently in the corner, their faces hidden in the shadows and the folds of their ragged clothes. Miríl beckoned to Arun, who stepped out of the darkness and removed the cowl from her head.

'Now do you believe him, old woman?' Arun spat the words out. 'This is what the Panjistri do!'

Tanyel blanched at the sights of Arun's translucent skin and her nerves and veins which pounded and throbbed with rage. Arun waved her gun threateningly before her; Tanyel stepped back in alarm and reached for Miríl's arm.

'An abomination,' she said, so softly that only Miríl heard her.

'No, Tanyel, the truth.'

Tanyel collected herself rapidly and addressed Arun. 'Whatever you are, you have nothing to do with me.'

Before Arun could reply Kraz stepped out of the shadows. He walked slowly towards Tanyel, who looked at him strangely.

She averted her eyes as she saw the scars and blisters on his face, but then something made her turn back. Kraz smiled crookedly and held out a burnt, peeling hand in greeting.

'Hello, Tanyel.'

Tanyel's eyes narrowed as she took in the sight of the monster before her. The proud face, still handsome despite its scars, the hair, once black and thick but now white and wispy, recalled a far-distant memory to her. She frowned as long-controlled emotions struggled to overcome the Panjistri's conditioning.

As Tanyel took a step towards him, Miríl too remembered where he had seen the surgeon before.

'Kraz?' The word fell leaden from Tanyel's lips.

Kraz nodded sadly and backed away. But Tanyel moved close to him, and he winced as she delicately touched his blisters and scars.

'You were so handsome once,' she said wonderingly. 'How did this happen to you?'

'The Panjistri,' he replied. 'They may have twisted and destroyed our bodies, but they distorted and stole your minds.'

Tanyel continued to stroke his face fondly, and gazed at him wide-eyed. 'I remember I was so proud of you when you went to work for the Panjistri. On that day you were so beautiful; I thought there was no one luckier than me. And then ... and then ...' She frowned as she tried in vain to recapture her lost memories. 'And then ... Why did I forget you?'

The room was silent; even Arun and Ace didn't dare say a word as the old woman tried to come to terms with a world which had just been turned upside down.

She looked back at Miríl and then to Ace. 'All you have told me is true?'

'Every word of it,' said Ace softly, suddenly aware of what Tanyel was going through.

Tanyel took a deep breath and something within her seemed to snap. 'Then the Panjistri shall not be allowed to deceive us for one moment longer,' she stated flatly.

With a last look at Kraz she strode determinedly out of the room. Before Ace could ask Miríl where she had gone the night-time quiet of the seminary buildings was shattered

136

by the repeated clanging of a loud bell. A thrill coursed through Miríl's body.

Tanyel, who had obeyed the Panjistri all her life, never quite understanding why she could not feel love for another person, now saw the truth. The worm had turned

Now she was arousing the seminary of Kirith from centuries of blind and unquestioning obedience.

'Kraz was her lover, it seems, all those years ago,' Raphael explained to Ace, as they sat waiting in Tanyel's rooms. 'But once he had left, the *zavát* made her forget.'

'Who'd have thought it of her? She seemed the proper ice queen,' whistled Ace. 'And now she's called all the teachers together in the great library.'

'You had a lot to do with it, Ace.'

Ace looked at him enquiringly. 'What do you mean?'

'You and the Doctor have thrown everything into doubt, made us think for ourselves for the first time in years.'

'I always caused trouble, even at school,' she said cheerfully. 'Did I ever tell you about the time I almost blew up the art room?'

He laughed. 'There's never been anyone on Kirith quite like you. Are there any more of you back in Peri-vale?'

'Nah, I'm the only one. Who'd have the nerve to make two of me?'

'I'm glad.'

They sat in silence for a while; and then Raphael ventured: 'Ace, if we ever get out of this would you . . . do you think the Doctor would let me come with you?'

Ace hesitated. 'You'd better ask him,' she said awkwardly. 'But if you want to go tramping around the cosmos I don't see why not.'

'That isn't the only reason, you know . . .'

The door opened suddenly, and Miríl regarded them with a knowing eye. He coughed loudly. Ace stood up sharply from the couch where she had been sitting with Raphael.

'Ace, you wouldn't happen to have any more of your hiccoughs in Paradise, would you?'

Ace looked blankly at him, until Raphael explained.

'No, sunshine-features here used up the last of them,' she said proudly. 'Why?'

'It's been decided that we will confront Lord Huldah with our demand that production of *zavát* should stop immediately, and that all allegations against the Panjistri are examined,' he said. 'If he refuses we will destroy the *zavát* production plant ourselves.'

Ace sighed, and stood up. 'And you think that slimeball's going to listen to you?'

'I pressed for more direct action but −'

Ace cut him short. 'You've got to strike now, when he's least prepared.'

'Then what would you suggest?'

'Get Joe Public on our side.' She thought for a moment. 'Where's the *zavát* produced?'

'At the Harbours, as you saw,' he said. 'It's then piped overland where it's processed and refined and then distributed.'

'And where's it distributed from?'

'The Council House; computers calculate the amount needed by every person for each day.'

Ace brightened and strode purposefully to the door. 'Well, are you coming or not?' she asked in mock irritation.

'Where to?'

'The Council House, of course,' she said brightly. 'Come on. I can't start a revolution all on my own, you know!'

Revna looked bleary-eyed at the Lord Procurator Huldah as he strode restlessly about his offices. She had never seen her master so agitated before. Tanyel's call to assembly had

138

awoken Huldah and many other Kirithons, who now wondered nervously why the bell, which tolled only on festival days, had been sounded in the dead of night.

He stopped by a window and pointed out into the night, down to the seminary building. Lights were blazing in every window and casement; the massive oak doors had been closed and bolted for the first time in living memory.

'What is happening down there, Revna?' he asked. 'Why are the teachers turning their place of learning into a fortress?'

In all matters save one Revna could read people like a book. And although his voice was steady she still detected the fearful apprehension that gripped the Lord Procurator's heart. Not without a slight feeling of satisfaction she realized that he was frightened. Things were slipping slowly out of his control.

'Can we not see into the seminary, Lord?' she asked.

Huldah indicated a bank of monitor screens on the far wall. 'Dead, every blasted one of them,' he said angrily.

'Ace,' guessed Revna and was filled with loathing.

Huldah agreed. 'Only she could identify and disconnect our concealed cameras. The others wouldn't even recognize them for what they are.'

'The secret entrances?' As a member of Huldah's retinue Revna knew that the entire town of Kirith was honey-combed with secret underground passages.

'Every one leading to the seminary is blocked,' he replied, wondering how the teachers could have known of them. It was impossible for such as Huldah to imagine the curiosity of the young Miríl as he explored his home town, or indeed to understand Tanyel, who had known about the passageways for years, but had chosen not to reveal their existence until now.

'What can we do, Huldah?' asked Revna, and noted with interest that her master was so preoccupied that he did not register her informal use of his name.

'I have informed Lord Reptu,' Huldah said. 'There is nothing we can do yet. Nothing, that is, but wait.'

Involuntarily his eyes looked up at Kirith's two moons and he mouthed a silent prayer.

Huldah was wrong. Not all the passages leading into the seminary had been blocked; one, forgotten by everyone except Raphael (who had used it once as a boy to get to the Council House and there drop a few home-made stink bombs), was still open. It was through this that Ace and Miríl were hurrying, even as Tanyel, Raphael, Arun and Kraz debated the next course of action with the teachers assembled in the great library.

'This isn't the safest of times to be conducting a raid on the Council House,' complained Miríl as he led Ace through the half-light of the tunnel. 'Just why do we need to go there anyway?'

'I told you,' Ace said brightly. 'I've got a plan.'

Miríl sighed. 'I wish you would tell me what it is.'

'Later,' she promised.

They reached a door which Ace pushed open warily. 'There's no one about,' she whispered and stepped out into a small cluttered storeroom. 'Where are all the guards?'

'We don't need them. Everyone on Kirith is trusted implicitly,' Miríl said ironically.

God knows how you lot would manage on Cup Final night in the West End, Ace said to herself. 'It's too quiet,' she remarked aloud as Miríl led her up a flight of stairs and on to a broad landing.

'It is the middle of the night, Ace,' Miríl reminded her, and opened a door. 'This is the place you wanted.'

They entered a brightly-lit room, empty except for row upon row of desktop computers and printers noisily

140

spewing out reams of information.

'This is serious stuff,' said Ace, as she inspected the nearest model. 'Much more advanced than the ones you use.'

She flipped through the plastic-covered pages of a huge file. 'These are programming instructions,' she said. 'I thought you didn't know how to program?'

'We've no need to,' Miríl said defensively. 'Everything is controlled from here.'

'But who programs and intializes the computers?'

'Huldah and his immediate circle program the machines and ensure that all our needs are met.'

'Revna too?'

Miríl nodded. Ace made a pretence of looking through the file and then said casually, 'Why does she hate me so much?'

'You're different from everyone else here; Revna hates that, and the effect that you have on men like Raphael.' He smiled. 'Even I, as an old man, have noticed that.'

Ace coloured and changed the subject. It was time to put her plan into operation. She tossed the programming manual onto a desk: she'd found the access codes she needed.

'The Kirithons trust the Panjistri because they provide them with all they need, right? Their food, their light, their heat?'

'Yes.'

'And if anything goes wrong, the *zavát* − which is their main source of food − guarantees that they forget and remain placid?'

'You know all that, Ace.'

'So what would happen if something went wrong with their food source?'

The idea had never occurred to Miríl. He looked at Ace with newly found admiration. 'What do you suggest?'

141

Ace sat down at a keyboard and made a great display of flexing her fingers like a pianist about to play a piece of music.

'Miss Sydenham in Computer Studies always said I had untapped skills,' she said. 'Half the time we ended up playing Space Invaders though . . . But there was one thing I was really mega-brilliant at. Want to know what it was?'

'I shudder to think, Ace. What was it?'

'Wiping programs!' she replied and gave Miríl a malevolent grin.

Hours passed, and a bright cold day dawned over Kirith. In his personal quarters, Huldah picked thoughtfully at a breakfast of meat and eggs as he waited for the message from the Panjistri. Over the video link from Kandasi the Lord Reptu had told him to calm himself. The Earthchild had now been located; let her remain in the seminary. All would be well, he assured him.

The Panjistri were so superior, so damned rational, fumed Huldah, that at times they underestimated the creatures to whom they were so insufferably generous. Like gods they presided over life on Kirith without ever once understanding the passions and furies which drove the people living on that planet.

The Doctor was dangerous, both to the Panjistri and to Huldah's power base on Kirith. Huldah knew that and that was why he had tried to kill him. But especially now that the Doctor was on Kandasi Island and safely out of the way Ace was even more of a threat. If she was so important to the Panjistri's mysterious plan, let them take her now; every moment she spent in Kirith threatened his rule. Let the Panjistri deal with matters of cosmic importance, while he, Huldah, got on with the job of running Kirith.

The door opened and Revna walked in, carrying a batch of reports. Huldah looked up from his breakfast.

'It's customary to knock, Revna,' he said sourly.

Revna stiffened for a moment and then apologized. 'I have just received dreadful news, my lord,' she began.

Huldah came round the table, and snatched the papers from her hand. As he read them his face darkened.

No one on Kirith had received their morning supplies of *zavát*-based foods; afternoon supplies had been hit, too. In addition, temporary electrical blackouts were occurring in parts of the town. Already a few brave citizens were complaining and asking questions.

'How did this happen?' he demanded.

'The programs for *zavát* distribution and power supply have been tampered with,' explained Revna calmly. 'Some programs have been corrupted, others totally destroyed.'

'That insufferable child!' barked the Lord Procurator of Kirith. 'How did she get into the computer room?'

Revna shrugged her shoulders, a little too nonchalantly, thought Huldah.

'Distribution must recommence immediately.'

'The machines will all have to be reprogrammed, my lord,' she continued. 'The girl destroyed our backup systems as well. It will take several days.'

'Then see to it immediately, Revna.'

'I was awaiting your instructions, my lord,' replied Revna.

'Then do it now!'

'At once,' she said. 'In the meantime, might I suggest that some of our meat and drink be given to the people?'

'Just go, Revna.'

As she left Revna smiled to herself. She hadn't disclosed the fact that she had received the reports of Ace's interference some hours ago, and had kept the news to herself until now. If Lord Huldah's position was in danger of being undermined, Revna was determined that she was going to use it to her best advantage.

143

It was late afternoon in the seminary. Ace looked out of a narrow window at the people in the streets below. She turned back to Miríl.

'It's still too quiet,' she said. 'Everyone outside just seems to be wandering about in a daze.'

'You've got to remember that they've always been provided for before,' he said. 'Now they've got no food, no heat, and when night comes they'll find they'll have very little light.'

'I feel sorry for them,' said Raphael.

'They'll have to fend for themselves,' said Arun unsympathetically. 'It's what the Unlike have been doing for years.'

'They'll also start to remember,' said Raphael. 'Couldn't they be spared that?'

Arun snorted mockingly. 'Tanyel has organized parties of teachers to go out and tell the people the truth,' she said.

'Will they believe them?' asked Ace doubtfully.

'You'd be surprised what hunger makes you do,' she said. 'And Kraz will go with them — they'll have to believe their own eyes.'

'Aren't you going too?'

'My people are still dying on the Darkfell,' she said. 'They need the Doctor's help.' She looked around at Ace, Miríl and Raphael. 'We are going to make another attempt on the Harbours. We are going to Kandasi.'

As night fell the only illumination in Kirith town came from the flickering lights of candles, and the steady electric glow from the Council House, which had its own generator. A sharp wind blew through the streets of the town.

Another hour passed and more lights appeared as bonfires were lit and people sat around them for comfort and warmth. They discussed the state of affairs. Many blamed Lord Huldah; some even spoke critically of the

144

Panjistri. Most, however, were convinced that nothing was seriously wrong. Everything would be all right in the morning.

Another hour passed. Rumours buzzed around of a creature swathed in rags and telling strange stories about the forbidden region of the Darkfell. Some said that the creature was accompanied by one of the teachers; some even said the teacher was Tanyel, who, for all her coolness, was still one of the most popular and respected figures in the town.

Another hour slipped by into the dead of night. An old woman was found dead in her apartment, her body frozen. A fight broke out between two young men over an apple; people turned away, not wishing to become involved. Others began to look enviously over at the bright warm lights shining in the Council House windows.

Another hour passed. People began hearing stories of horrors at the Harbours. A serious-looking young man criticized the Panjistri and Huldah; some older people urged him to be quiet; many others nodded their heads in agreement. At the foot of the town sparks from a bonfire set alight the thatched roof of a small house. It was almost half an hour before someone had the presence of mind to organize a chain gang to bring water from the river.

Another hour passed. A baby awoke, bawling in its mother's arms. The mother looked at it helplessly, unsure what to do: her stomach was rumbling as much as her child's. In the end, unable to look after it, she left the child crying in her apartment. In the streets outside a man stopped her. 'My fiancée,' he said with tears in his eyes. 'Have you seen her? Her name is Kareena. She's a dancer . . .'

A final hour passed. In the Council House Huldah ensured that all the doors and entrances were barred and sealed. In the distance he could see a stream of people,

145

holding aloft flaming torches, marching up to the Council House.

As Revna entered his offices a brick smashed through the window, showering his early morning breakfast of freshly-caught fish with shards of bright shining glass.

Chapter 14

Feel the power and the ecstasy of power, coursing and throbbing through me.

The joy of dissonance, and the jumbled lights of chaos and uncertainty. It fills my being like nothing before; I feel invigorated, refreshed, reborn. Awake.

Wonderful, glorious unpredictability, scarred and confused; anger and joy rising together as one.

Such great power, and even greater purpose. Shining like ever-changing lights in a wonderful kaleidoscope of never-before-seen colours.

It is ... exciting.

And brings me further to my apotheosis.

Distant, beckoning lights flared and coalesced around the scruffy little man as he spun head over heels, his coattails flapping in the wind of a colourless void.

Humans say that at the moment of death all one's past experiences flit before the eyes. How right they were, thought the little man. Even though his life was far, far from over, this transmigration of his being into another form was a kind of death, and brought with it its own type of reckoning.

Passing before him were the faces of all the friends he had made in his past incarnation. They had all gone now to carry on their own lives while he continued on, a lonely wanderer through the vastness of time. Ben and Polly. Shy, frightened Victoria. Even Jamie and Zoe.

Jamie and Zoe. The Time Lords had returned them to their own time zones, to seventeenth-century Scotland and to a space station in the twenty-first century. His masters had said that they would remember nothing of him but the first adventure they had shared — that, and nothing more.

Poppycock, thought the little man even as the first excruciating pains of enforced regeneration shot mercilessly through his body. Self-satisfied and secure in their soulless citadels, the Time Lords understood nothing of the human spirit.

Everyone the little man had ever met had been changed in some way or another by his presence: it was part of the reason of his being, was both his blessing and his curse. After all, he was the Doctor.

The final tremors of regeneration thudded cruelly through him, and for that one fleeting half-instant his mind was opened, and his entire past and future shone, cruel and clear, before him.

Everything gets old and falls apart in time. It even happens to me. But most things can be fixed. Let's see what I can do.

His eyes snapped open, and he found he was trembling at his unthinking folly. Unconsciousness began to descend upon him, but before he could pass out and forget, he knew what he had to do.

Chapter 15

The Doctor looked up apprehensively at the massive granite buildings which formed the Skete of Kandasi, all of them featureless and functional apart from the ornate death's head which crowned each one. There was no sign of life anywhere.

He switched on his radiation detector which, as before, was beeping furiously. Suddenly the sound changed to a high-pitched whine which almost deafened him. He switched it off hurriedly and read the readings displayed on the LCD counter.

For several moments it had detected an inordinate rush of artron energy, which had now levelled off to the 'normal' levels for this planet. The Doctor looked up thoughtfully at the arrow-shaped aeriel which towered above him on the summit of the hill.

A loud crash and creaking of doors make him hurry behind a corner and duck for cover.

Streaming down from the buildings at the top of the hill came a band of forty or so Companions, all tall and heavily armed and chattering excitedly amongst themselves. They marched directly towards a fleet of three silver craft which lay at the foot of the hill.

Following them were six old men and women, dressed in long flowing habits and skullcaps. Their faces were fixed and stern, and they were silent as they walked down to the three waiting cars.

At last, the Panjistri, thought the Doctor, and as the air cars rose and sped off down towards the harbour, he wondered what had finally brought them to Kirith.

As the day had progressed in Kirith town so more and more of the people had been convinced by the words of Tanyel and her fellow teachers. When Kraz had returned from the Darkfell and brought back with him several of the Unlike, the Kirithons could finally see with their own eyes the price they had had to pay for the life of ease the Panjistri had given them.

And yet it was not just the unmasking of the true nature of the Panjistri which fired their passion and anger. For the first time in centuries, the people of Kirith were hungry.

Zavát was their lifeline; it was provided for them on a daily basis in all its different forms. They had become so dependent on their regular supply that they had never thought of storing it; nor had they ever learnt to grow and cultivate efficiently fruit and vegetables.

Now, after only a day of being deprived of food, their stomachs were empty and they were beginning to panic, wondering where their next meal was coming from. The thought of Lord Huldah and his cronies, secure in the Council House, dining on fresh meats and vegetables made them even angrier.

Tanyel and Kraz had elected not to reveal the main constituent of the Kirithons' staple diet: the knowledge that for centuries the Kirithons had been eating the reprocessed remains of their own people would have been too much for many to bear.

Some of those with stronger, more free-thinking minds

were also beginning to remember the things which the *zavát* had conveniently helped them to forget. People began to question the disappearance of loved ones and relatives; some older people, like Miríl before them, wondered why they had no memory of their parents or grandparents.

There were, however, those who clung tightly to their blind unquestioning faith in the Panjistri. These were not just the ones who had gained most from the Matriarch's people; they were also timid, honest folk who feared the future and were contented to carry on with the comfortable life they had always known.

What if the Panjistri did experiment on a few misfits and low-lifes? At least they fed them well.

While these people stayed in their homes waiting for the storm of dissent to abate, others climbed the road leading to where the throng gathered in the square before the Council House, shouting their demands up to the Brethren.

In a high window the burly figure of Huldah looked nervously out. The crowd jeered and demanded that he come out and speak to them.

Huldah turned back to Revna. 'Something must be done soon, my lord,' she said.

'Don't you think I don't know that!' he snapped. 'When will food supplies be restored?'

Revna checked her files. 'Several days,' she said flatly. 'All the programs were lost when Ace wiped the systems.'

She neglected to mention that she had deliberately delayed the start of the reprogramming by several hours. Huldah had lost touch in his later days; he wouldn't notice.

Huldah looked bemused. 'I've done so much for them, Revna, ensured that they got the best of everything. I loved them like my own children. Why are they now turning against me?'

Perhaps because the only person you've ever loved was

151

yourself. And loyalty's not an attractive option when your stomach is empty, thought Revna. 'What will you do, lord?' she asked.

'I don't know,' he said despairingly, and tried once more to contact Kandasi on the video link-up. The screen was filled with static.

'What should I do, Panjistri, what should I do?'

Revna looked at the Lord Procurator with thinly veiled disdain.

Ace, Raphael, Arun and Miríl crouched behind a heather-topped hillock near the Harbours watching the Panjistri and the Companions disembark from the hovercraft. The Companions already stationed at the Harbours welcomed them.

'I've never seen the Panjistri arrive in such force before,' said Miríl. 'What are they doing here?'

'Obvious, isn't it?' said Ace. 'Huldah's called them in to put down the unrest.'

'We've got to get back then,' said Raphael, instinctively rising to his feet. 'Tanyel will need our help.'

Arun pulled him roughly down again. 'Do you want to get us shot?' she said. 'We go on to Kandasi.'

'We have to find the Professor, Raphael,' said Ace as he began to protest. 'He's the only one who can help us.'

Meekly Raphael agreed.

For the second night the people of Kirith had had no food, heat or light. Attempts had been made to break down the doors of the Council House, but, like those of the seminary, the massive doors had been built to withstand even the strongest attack.

Still Huldah had not come out to speak to his people, despite their insistence. He sat in his offices, unblinking, stunned at his subjects' volte-face. There was a large part of Huldah that truly believed that everything he had done was for the good of the Kirithons; if he could also do himself and his friends good along the way, then what of it? Their rebellion was simply beyond his comprehension.

Stripped of his power and apparently without the support and guiding light of Reptu and the Panjistri, the Lord Huldah was a lost man.

Revna meanwhile was supervising the reprogramming of all the computers, allowing none of the programmers rest until their task was finished. They worked like automata, scarcely understanding what they were doing and merely following the instructions taught to them by the Panjistri years ago.

She returned to Huldah to report on the progress and found him once again standing at the window. This time, however, there was joy and relief on his face. He urged her to look.

Down below in the streets pandemonium reigned. People were scattering in all directions, screaming and howling in disbelief, as forty armed Companions rushed into the square from each side, firing their bullets aimlessly into the crowd.

Kirithons pushed each other aside in their blind panic, showing no respect for age or infirmity as they ran to save their own lives. All over the square people were dropping, blood, brains and guts tumbling from their bodies as the Companions' bullets and shells hit them; others scrambled over their corpses to seek refuge in the tiny adjacent streets.

The six Panjistri followed, their faces sombre and unfeeling as they surveyed the carnage and watched the crowd disperse.

A gang of Kirithons, more foolhardy than the rest, attempted to confront one of the Companions. A female Panjistri raised a hand, and a chunk of masonry detached itself from a nearby building, crushing to death both the

Companion and its attackers.

One Kirithon, running blindly into another Panjistri, watched in horror as the seemingly frail old man crushed his arm into a bloody pulp.

Within minutes it was over, an efficient and coldly emotionless extermination of those who had dared to defy the Panjistri. There was no trace of triumph in their faces: it was simply a job that had to be done.

As the smoke cleared, the six Panjistri beckoned their Companions to follow them to the Council House, whose doors Huldah had already ordered to be opened. Behind them they left a pile of corpses and the bitter metallic smell of freshly spilt blood.

Disgusting, thought Revna as she turned away from the window and the bile rose in her throat.

Ace and her three companions looked warily around the hovercraft which the Panjistri had left in the bay. Like the Harbours, it too, was empty; the Panjistri had seen no reason to put a guard on it.

'Do you know how to work this thing?' asked Ace.

Arun returned from examining the controls in the small cabin. 'I saw the Panjistri operate it when I worked here. I understand the basics, yes,' she replied.

'Well, what are we waiting for? Let's go!'

Tentatively, Arun touched the controls. Gently the engines thrummed into life, and the hovercraft moved slowly out of the Harbours, its destination the island of Kandasi.

Right into the lion's den, thought Ace.

Within minutes of their entering the Council House the Panjistri had instructed that the Brethren should not leave the building. The armed Companions were put on guard to protect them from any further insurrection.

154

Ignoring the effusive greetings of Huldah, the six Panjistri immediately demanded that Revna lead them up to the computer rooms, where they then coolly dismissed her programmers. Revna stood back open-mouthed as she marvelled at the skill and the speed with which they reprogrammed and restored all the programs which Ace had destroyed.

Within half an hour lights all over Kirith blazed back on. In the vaults of the Council House the distribution machines responsible for *zavát* whirred and clunked back into life.

A Panjistri looked up from his terminal. 'All will be as it was before,' he stated coldly. 'Your power systems are now running as they should; food supplies will be resumed within the hour.

Revna bowed her head in thanks. 'I am grateful for the great munificence of —' she began.

'Thanks are unnecessary,' interrupted the Panjistri. 'Your welfare is all that concerns us. Now please lead us to the Lord Procurator Huldah.'

Revna led them to Huldah's office, where the Lord Procurator welcomed them once again. He wrung his hands obsequiously.

'We are eternally grateful for your opportune intervention, my lords ...' he began, but the Panjistri silenced him.

'The Earthchild has eluded your grasp again, Huldah, putting our entire mission in great danger.'

'But I —'

'The revolt should never have been allowed to progress this far.'

'But I tried to contact you, he pleaded. 'The communications systems were not working!'

'We entrusted you with great power. You have abused that in pandering to your own whims and desires and not

155

caring for the people as you should.'

'But haven't I carried out all your plans?'

'The people distrust you, Huldah; that lack of faith in you destabilizes Kirith and endangers our mission. Therefore we have no further use for you.'

Huldah's face turned white as he realized he was being made a scapegoat. He trembled uncontrollably as the six Panjistri surrounded him. He looked over to Revna, who was standing in the doorway. 'Revna, help me.'

Revna turned her face away.

The eyes of the Panjistri, usually so weak and misty grey, glowed with green fire.

Huldah screamed in horrible agony.

When the Panjistri stepped aside there was nothing left of Huldah but a boiling, steaming grey glob of matter.

The Panjistri walked to the door, but before leaving stopped and turned to Revna.

'Revna. You were right in contacting us when you did. Huldah obviously thought he could deal with the situation on his own.'

'At your service, my lords,' she said, feeling in her pocket for the circuit she had stolen from the video link, thereby ensuring that Huldah couldn't contact his masters himself.

'The Companions are to remain here to ensure that never again will such a calamity occur.'

'Of course.'

'We leave now for Kandasi. Let us not have to come to Kirith under such circumstances again.'

'I assure you all will be well.'

'Farewell − Lord Procurator Revna.'

A new day dawned on Kirith town. In the square the bodies had been cleared away. People awoke as though from a bad dream, scarcely believing what had happened. Some said that it had indeed been nothing but a dream, some sort of mass hallucination. Most preferred not to think about it.

But some people remembered and looked at their neighbours in a slightly different light, reminding themselves exactly what role they had played in the great debacle of the previous night.

Revna declared a general amnesty. Such was the generosity of the Panjistri that all transgressions would be forgiven and forgotten; the people of Kirith were blessed with the most understanding of rulers.

A feast day was declared. The seminarians, now halved in number, rang the great bell, calling the people to the festival. Wine flowed and mountains of food were consumed. A wonderful joyous time was had by all.

The people of Kirith had everything they could ever ask for.

And life was good.

The noise of the celebrations reached even to the Darkfell, where Tanyel, Kraz and others who had escaped the massacre had sought refuge with the Unlike. They looked at each other grimly. They had each other now. The first battle was over; they were determined it would not be the last.

Chapter 16

Arun was surprised at how easily she handled the hover-craft. It sped over the rough sea like a dream, bringing them closer every second to the terrible stronghold of Kandasi. Perhaps, she thought, it had something to do with its construction; perhaps the 'living' metal it was made of ensured a trouble-free journey.

Ace joined Miríl, who was on the deck, busy throwing up over the side. He looked up embarrassed. 'I do apologize,' he said. 'I'm unused to sea journeys. Forbidden, you see.'

Ace grinned; there was something very likeable about the fallible old man. Raphael certainly trusted and loved him as a substitute for the father he had lost. She wondered about the circumstances of his parents' death: had they also been sacrificed to the Panjistri? Perhaps they'd never know.

Raphael was looking out apprehensively at Kandasi: they had left the Harbours almost twenty minutes ago and were fast approaching the shore.

'I'm frightened, Ace,' he said.

She rested her hand on his. 'We're all scared witless, sunshine; but we each hide it in different ways. Look at

Arun, putting the boot in and barking orders. Miríl, making a joke out of it.'

'And you? How do you hide it?'

'It's all in a day's work for me,' she lied.

'I can't believe that,' he said. 'You must be frightened of something.'

'Probably of being found out,' she said cryptically. Before Raphael could pursue his uncomfortable line of questioning the sea on the port side exploded in a shower of spume and the craft lurched violently to the right, throwing them all to the deck.

'What are you playing at, Arun!' Ace shouted at the stunned pilot.

Arun started to disclaim all responsibility when Raphael pointed out at the sea.

'Bloody hell, it's Godzilla!' yelled Ace.

Having trailed them almost since they left the Harbours, the sea lizard, yet another of the Panjistri's genetic mutations, excited by the scent of fresh blood, had chosen this moment to strike.

Its lithe neck, as thick as a tree trunk, smashed out of the water and bore down on the craft. Saliva drooled from its open mouth as it gnashed greedily at the humans twenty metres below it. Rows of serrated teeth glistened in the sunlight. Its ribbed gills opened and closed as it neared the peak of its excitement and prepared to strike.

Arun scrambled over the deck, grabbed her gun and fired at the creature. The shots merely glanced off its armour-plated hide, doing it no damage; the noise served only to irritate it even more.

Beneath the water it flicked its tail, almost capsizing the boat; Arun was flung against the starboard side, landing with a sickening *thunk*. As the boat tipped and turned in the water, Ace staggered over to the controls to try to steady the craft in the turbulent waters.

Sliding and slipping on the wet deck Raphael tried to reach Ace as the monster spied him and with a bellow of lust and greed bore down on him.

'Raphael!' Ace left the controls and ran towards him as he stood transfixed in the creature's basilisk glare.

Miríl was quicker. His seasickness forgotten, his one thought now was the safety of his former ward. He darted over and wrested the gun from the hands of the still-dazed Arun.

Adrenalin coursed through his body, giving him additional strength and speed to run over to Raphael and place himself between him and the gaping maw of the dragon. With a hand which had never before been so steady he fired the gun straight into the creature's two fearsome eyes.

It screeched and buckled away, shards of white-hot pain reaching and convulsing its tiny brain. For a second it dived beneath the water, thrashing about in its agony. Then it shot out of the sea again and in literally blind fury it bore down once more on the boat.

Its jaws clamped down hard on Miríl as it snatched him from the deck and took him, struggling and screaming in the air. The gun fell from his grasp into the sea.

Ace and Raphael watched in helpless horror as the creature dragged the still struggling bloody form of Miríl away from the ship. There was nothing they could do but hope that Miríl's pain would end. With a whoop of triumph the creature dived with its prey deep into the black waters.

The sea calmed as if nothing had happened and the hovercraft sped swiftly on its way.

For a long time there was no sound, only the despairing, uncomprehending sobs of Raphael as he lay cradled in Ace's comforting arms.

Curiouser and curiouser, thought the Doctor as he

160

wandered around the buildings which made up the Skete of Kandasi. Most of them were merely storehouses, containing nothing but stocks of grain and provisions destined for the Brethren in Kirith, or spare electronic parts for not particularly sophisticated machinery. One smaller building served as a maintenance shed for the air cars which the Panjistri had used for getting down to the beach; another contained some rudimentary agricultural equipment.

Apart from that the settlement was as dead and lonely as the grave; people had not lived here for years. So where were all the Panjistri? Had they all gone to Kirith, or were they in hiding somewhere on this forbidden island?

The Doctor sauntered up to the building at the top of the hill. The conductor for the artron energy seemed to wink enticingly at him in the sunshine.

'Now why would they need artron energy?' he said. 'What do you think, Brigadier?'

He stopped and slapped his forehead. I am the Doctor and I am living in my own present, he repeated to himself. The Brigadier and all the others belong to the past which is gone!

He shook his head worriedly and walked on. A strange haunting melody suddenly broke the silence. Somehow it sounded very familiar.

The Doctor's eyes darted frantically around trying to locate its source. He frowned: he recognized that sound.

It was the sound of someone playing a recorder.

Arun guided the hovercraft into a safe landing on the north side of the island, rather than at the southern harbour, reasoning that the more secret their arrival the better.

Her navigation past the sharp needle rocks on that side of the island surprised even herself; she again wondered just what help she might have had from the 'living' metal

161

from which the boat was supposedly constructed. The outlying buildings of the Skete lay only an hour's walk away.

As they disembarked Raphael looked disconsolately out at sea, the last resting place of his old friend. His eyes were raw and red with crying, as he remembered all the slights he had made Miríl, and all the things that had been left unsaid. He felt a cold clammy hand on his shoulder.

'He was a brave man, Raphael,' Arun said kindly. 'He raised you well. But there is nothing we can do for him now.'

'It feels heartless just leaving him out there.'

'There is nothing we can do,' she repeated, this time more sternly, and walked away.

Ace came over and took his hand. 'Come on, Raphael, we have to go on.'

'When I think of all that he did for me, and all the thanks I showed,' he muttered. 'Ace, I feel so alone.'

'We can't go back. We can only go forward: that's what the Professor taught me,' she said. 'You'll have to see the stars for Miríl now.'

Raphael grasped her hand tightly as though he were a child scared that its mother might leave it. 'I need you here now, Ace. I can't do it all by myself.'

'No one ever said they needed me before,' she said awkwardly.

'Not even the Doctor?'

Arun interrupted them brusquely. 'We are here for a purpose, you remember? My people are still dying. We have to find the Doctor.'

'Well, you certainly took your time in getting here, old chap!'

The Doctor stared in amazement at the ghostlike figure of the scruffy little man who was sitting cross-legged on the ground, looking for all the world like a mischievous pixie.

'What are you doing here?' the Doctor spluttered.

The other man finished the tune he was playing on his recorder, and then leapt to his feet.

'Well, strictly speaking, I'm not really here at all,' he said airily as he began to fade in and out of vision. 'Not in substance anyway. I'm just a figment of your imagination, your guilty conscience if you like.'

'You've no right to be here at all,' protested the Doctor.

'Well, if you'd have paid attention to the messages I was trying to send through the TARDIS's telepathic circuits, I wouldn't need to be,' the Doctor's second incarnation said to him grumpily. 'But you're so high and mighty these days you won't realize that you might have made a mistake.'

'What are you prattling on about?'

'There's no need to be so superior with me, you know,' said the second Doctor, and looked meaningfully down at his successor, who was even smaller than himself. Then his mood changed. 'I've — we've been used.'

'Don't be ridiculous,' snapped the Doctor, but there was a troubled expression on his face.

'Aha!' crowed the other. 'You've suspected it too! It's not so nice when you're being manipulated as well, is it!'

'What d'you mean?'

'Well, look at poor old Ace,' he said. 'She trusts you, loves you even. And what do you do half of the time? Throw her into situations she just can't understand, use her as nothing more than a tool, a pawn in your little games. What's wrong? Don't you trust her? Afraid if you tell her everything she'll leave you? You know, I think you're getting a little bit above yourself, my friend.'

The Doctor winced uncomfortably under the accusation. His previous self continued: 'Now listen closely because

163

I don't have much time. You think you understand what's going on in Kirith, don't you? But you don't know the half of it. There's a greater evil afoot than even you realize. And you — I — we're responsible for it. Remember after we first regenerated? We were at our weakest then. We became — infected, if you like.'

The Doctor's eyes narrowed as he listened.

'The TARDIS landed on a planet. There you — we — met a little girl. Do you remember her? Lovely sweet child, the apple of her parents' eyes; her name was Lilith.'

The Doctor nodded slowly as he tried to recall the hazy days following his first regeneration. Once again he saw the hopeful tear-stained face of the little girl who asked him to mend her doll.

'Well, that was five thousand years ago,' said the second Doctor. 'She's grown up a bit since then. Seems she now calls herself the Grand Matriarch.'

The Doctor stood alone, silently digesting all that his previous self could tell him before he had faded away. If what he said was true then the situation needed to be looked at in a totally different light. Suddenly a commotion behind him disturbed him, and he spun around.

'Professor!' cried Ace.

The Doctor looked at her warily, remembering her clone. 'Ace, is it really you?'

'Well, who'd you expect it to be?' she said affronted.

The Doctor's face beamed and he hugged his companion. 'Ace! You've no idea how I've missed you! Are you all right?'

'Now that we've escaped the Lock Ness Monster, yeah.'

'Lo*ch*,' corrected the Doctor and then listened as Ace introduced Arun, and told him of their adventures. He showed genuine grief at the news of Miríl's death.

'Will you cure my people, Doctor?' asked Arun, as

practical as ever.

'Once I've tracked down the Panjistri,' he answered. 'But where they can be I can't say.'

'Doctor, look over here.' Raphael had strayed from the others and had wandered over to a large hangar-like building a little way off. He opened the doors and the others followed him in.

'Of course,' said the Doctor as he viewed the inside of the structure. 'I should have guessed.'

The room within was as large as a football pitch and empty apart from enormous latticed panels at each of the four compass points, and a small control console, lights twinkling along its keyboard. Lining the walls, huge generators buzzed softly. The huge glass roof overhead gave them a magnificent view of the two moons which were now appearing in the darkening sky.

'What is it, Professor?'

'Remember what I told you about artron energy, Ace?'

'It's a force which helps power TARDISes, you said.'

'The Panjistri have harnessed it to operate a huge matter transporter.'

'This?' gasped Ace as she looked around the room. 'This is serious hardware, Professor. What have they been sending down here? An army?'

'How about an entire species?'

'What do you mean?'

Before the Doctor could answer, Raphael said: 'If this is some sort of transporter where does it go to?'

'Shall we find out?' the Doctor asked cheerily, and walked over to the control console. 'The coordinates are preset; let's see where we end up.'

He activated the console.

The four panels surrounding them crackled into activity and bathed them in a blazing blue light. The light seemed to creep into their very bones, chilling them to the marrow.

165

Each of them felt a quiet tugging at their bodies, and then all was blackness.

In a half-instant they had all blinked out of existence.

The Doctor rubbed his eyes in an attempt to clear his head. At his feet Ace, Raphael and Arun lay unconscious. He bent down to shake them awake.

Ace was the first to come to. 'Leave me alone,' she groaned as the Doctor helped her to her feet. 'I feel like the morning after at Greenford disco.'

'Not the most pleasant way to travel,' agreed the Doctor, and looked to Raphael and Arun, who were also sitting up.

'Where are we, Doctor?' asked Arun.

The Doctor looked about knowingly, taking in his surroundings. 'The home of the Panjistri,' he replied.

They were in a room similar to the one they had just left, the only difference being that one wall was, in truth, one vast window. 'Well, well, well. Now it's all starting to make a lot more sense.'

He pointed out through the panoramic window at the steady brilliant stars suspended in the vast blackness of space.

Down below, three hundred thousand miles way, the planet Kirith spun peacefully on its axis.

Chapter 17

At last completion is at hand! The one thing needed for my/our becoming whole is now within my awareness, within my sphere of influence!

My calls for him/her/it have reached across the vastness and have been heeded. Now my/our future is assured.

Soon nothing will be able to stand in my/our way for all will be within my/our power, a power that will know no bournes.

Events are now reaching their climax. And then when all the energies are taken and absorbed then will come my/our apotheosis!

It is only a matter of time.

'Where are we, Professor?' asked Ace.

'I told you. The home of the Panjistri.'

'But I always thought the Panjistri lived on Kandasi,' said Arun.

The Doctor shook his head. 'Nonono, that's merely a waystation, a point of transit.' He waved his arms about the room. 'This is the real Kandasi, a space station over three hundred thousand miles above the surface of Kirith.'

Raphael who had not said a word since arriving but had

instead continued to gaze out into space, turned back to the others. His eyes were afire with wonder and excitement.

'The stars — they're beautiful up here, but so different, so much more constant and steady.'

'No atmosphere,' explained Ace smugly, recalling her science classes. 'They don't twinkle because their light isn't diffused like it is down on the ground.'

'But Kirith has two moons,' he said. 'I can only see one.'

That stumped Ace. She looked to the Doctor for help.

'You're in the other one, Raphael,' he answered and the others looked at him disbelievingly.

'Come off it, Professor!'

The Doctor looked hurt. 'Kandasi is gigantic, Ace, over a thousand miles in diameter. It's made of a highly reflective metal; down on the planet it would look like a natural satellite.' He bent down to examine the nearest wall.

'I shouldn't wonder if it's the same living metal their seacraft are made of. Probably of a very high density too. The gravitational pull it exerts could account for the changeable climatic conditions down on Kirith.'

'But why do the Panjistri stay up here?' persisted Ace.

'Safety,' said Arun. 'Who could reach and attack them in space?'

'That's partly the reason,' said the Doctor. 'But the weightlessness of space could also provide the ideal environment for bio-genetic experiments of a very delicate nature.'

'Like what?' Ace demanded. Come on, Professor, don't you think it's time to tell us what you know? she thought.

The Doctor considered for a minute, and then looked thoughtfully at Raphael and Arun before continuing. 'Think about it. The greatest geneticists ever came here in Kandasi thousands of years ago to a dead and sterile planet. Since then a race developed on this planet, bypassing war and aggression and all the other trials that evolution throws at any other species.'

Ace frowned and looked at Arun and Raphael. Even Arun's blue-tinted skin had paled with a dawning realization.

'A perfect race —' he pronounced the words with irony — 'beautiful, happy, talented, healthy; even their wounds clear up in a few hours. But they're a people with no history: their ancient ruins are fakes, their histories are fabricated. Miríl couldn't remember his parents, and I bet Raphael never knew his grandparents. Because they never had any.'

'What are you saying, Doctor?' asked Arun, although she already knew the answer.

'You and Raphael, even Huldah, aren't Kirithons. All your ancestors were born and bred up here by the Panjistri and then sent down to the planet.' He pointed down to the brown sphere below him. 'Kirith isn't a civilization, or a Utopia of peace and harmony. It's nothing more than one giant laboratory experiment.'

He paused to gauge the reaction of Arun and Raphael. Arun was visibly shocked, but there was a strange tranquillity about Raphael. The Doctor clapped his hands together.

'Now,' he said, 'shall we go and meet our unwilling hosts?'

Reptu looked away from the video screens with irritation as Fetch entered the room.

'What is it?' he demanded wearily.

'Forgive me for disturbing you, my lord,' Fetch whimpered, 'but I am worried about my mistress.'

'The Matriarch?' asked Reptu. There was evident concern in his voice. 'What is wrong with her?'

'She paces her chamber continually and will not rest,' Fetch said, 'She is beginning to mutter strange words to herself, and is possessed of a new vigour.' A single tear fell from Fetch's eye. 'She has dismissed me from her service.'

Reptu raised a questioning eyebrow: he knew of the Matriarch's fondness for Fetch.

'She said she would no longer be held responsible for me. Said that I was to seek sanctuary down on the planet's surface. I sensed sadness in her voice; but when I protested she had me flung out of her rooms.'

As much as he found Fetch's presence distasteful, Reptu felt sympathy for the faithful servant. He nodded to the screens, on which the Doctor's party was shown leaving the transporter room.

'Five thousand years of waiting is finally at an end, Fetch. Apotheosis is within reach. Within hours our task will have been achieved,' he said. 'The Grand Matriarch has an awesome burden to bear; now, especially, she dare not be swayed by foolish emotions.' He smiled not unkindly. 'Rest assured that after today you will regain her favours. It is not the end, Fetch; it is the long-awaited New Beginning for us all.'

Ace had never been particularly afraid of heights, but crossing a narrow bridge which had no handrail, and which swayed worryingly over an abyss of several thousand feet, was enough to give her pause for thought. But as it was the only way across from the transporter room to the main part of Kandasi there was no alternative. Holding on to the Doctor and Raphael's hands, with Arun bringing up the rear, they edged slowly across.

There was no sound to be heard. The towers rising out of the abyss still throbbed with lights, but through the windows none of the Panjistri could be seen. When they reached the other side Ace remarked on this.

'So where's the welcoming committee?' she asked. 'This place is about as dead as a dodo.'

'It does have an abandoned feel to it,' agreed the Doctor quietly and raised a hand to touch his throat. Was it his imagination or was it getting hard to breathe?

'It's not dead though,' said Raphael and the other three looked at him. 'Can't you hear it?' he asked.

The others strained to hear the soft, pulsing sound resounding in the emptiness; it reminded them almost — but not quite — of a human heartbeat. That sound seemed to be accompanied by yet another, this time a sibilant seductive lilt, serving as a counterpoint to the dominant melody.

'It reminds me of something,' said Arun.

'It's a *koríntol*,' said Raphael evenly.

Spook city, thought Ace. That's all we need — a haunted space station!

The Grand Matriarch looked on greedily at the progress of the Doctor and Ace. Now at last the events which had been started five thousand years ago would reach their conclusion.

On a table by her side there glistened in the moonlight the helmet which had crowned so many Kirithon heads over the past centuries. Now it was waiting for its final recipient.

Soon the suffering of Lilith would be over, and the Grand Matriarch would know power, power unmatched since the beginning of time itself.

They had just begun to descend the stairway on the far side of the abyss when they received their first and only warning. Something thudded dully behind them. The Doctor looked back and saw the hull of Kandasi buckle

171

and begin to fall in on itself.

'Everyone down the stairs!' he cried, and sent his companions tumbling down the steps.

Ace gave forth a violent curse as she tumbled head first. From somewhere far off an alarm screeched as emergency precautions were automatically put into operation. Doors throughout the whole of Kandasi closed and sealed themselves off.

The Doctor's party looked on aghast as a whole portion of wall simply dissolved and opened out on to the void of outer space. Air whooshed out of the space station, sucking them out into the vacuum.

The windows in the towers burst and shattered, and flew towards the hole, showering them in lethal shards and slivers of glass.

Blinded by the shower of debris rushing towards the opening, the Doctor grabbed a handrail on the stairwell for support, and reached out to grab the hand of Arun, who was being slowly sucked out. A body thudded into them, and in vain they tried to catch Raphael as the outrush of air dragged him out into open space.

With aching and bloodied fingers Raphael tried to hold on to the edge of the steps to save himself. But the force of the wind was too strong; he made one last despairing effort to drag himself forwards and then felt the strength drain from his body. He moved inexorably towards the break in the hull.

And thudded against hard metal.

Dazed, he looked at the hull. There was no trace of a break; all around him air roared back into the room. On the staircase the Doctor was helping Arun to her feet.

A door slid open and Reptu stepped out. He looked down on them with a mixture of amusement and disdain.

'Thank you,' gasped the Doctor.

'It was nothing, merely a telepathic command,' said

Reptu.

'What happened?'

'Kandasi identified you as intruders so it defended itself, rearranging its molecular structure to send you into space.'

Reptu's tone hid his concern, not for the Doctor's wellbeing but at the event which had led up to Kandasi's act of self-defence. Normally the Grand Matriarch constantly kept the space station's living metal in check, regulating its every action. For Kandasi to have acted on its own initiative meant that she must have abnegated command; it had taken three of the Panjistri's most powerful telepaths to command the space station to seal the hole in the hull

'But there is no advantage in killing you three,' he continued.

'Ace!' cried the Doctor. 'Where's Ace?'

'Safe,' said Reptu equanimously. 'But you will never see her again.'

Raphael shook the old man by the shoulders. 'What do you mean? What have you done to her?'

Reptu seemed taken aback by Raphael's violence. 'She is joining the Grand Matriarch.'

'No.' The Doctor's voice was hard and full of menace.

'You don't understand, Doctor,' said Reptu. 'Without the Earthchild the whole Universe is doomed. What is her one life compared to countless billions? I appreciate your concern, Doctor, but the facts are simple: Ace must die so that the rest of creation may live.'

Chapter 18

Ace rubbed her aching head and looked around her. When Kandasi's hull had opened up she had grazed her head as the Doctor pushed her down the stairs and she'd been knocked unconscious. The space station's emergency systems had gone into operation, and the bottom of the stairs had been sealed off, effectively cutting her off from the Doctor and the others.

From somewhere nearby she vaguely heard a door slide open, and then felt a long gnarled hand helping her to her feet. 'Welcome to Kandasi, Earthchild,' said an ancient cracked voice.

Who are you calling Earthchild, Granny? she thought and looked up at the kindly smiling face of the old woman. She seemed to be genuinely concerned for her welfare.

'Let me help you to your feet,' she said. 'You've had a bit of a bump.'

For someone seemingly so frail, the old woman had no trouble in helping Ace up. 'Where's the Professor and Raphael?' Ace asked suspiciously.

'There was a nasty little accident back there,' tutted the woman, 'but don't worry, they're quite safe. I'll take you to them if you like.' She looked at Ace, who felt uncomfortable under the glare of her fiery green eyes. 'My name's Lilith. What's yours?'

'Ace . . .' Distrusting, but strangely compliant with the old woman's wishes, Ace allowed herself to be led away.

As she took the six-fingered bejewelled hand, she wondered why the old woman was shaking so much

'Tell us where Ace is, old man, or you die.'

Arun snapped the command while at the same time threatening to snap Reptu's neck which she held in a vice-hold. Reptu made no attempt to resist even though Raphael knew he could shrug off Arun as easily as swatting a fly.

'Why don't we let Reptu have his say?' suggested the Doctor, who was just as concerned for Ace but realized that threats would have no effect on any of the Panjistri.

Arun released her grip. 'Thank you,' Reptu said sarcastically, and made an exaggerated show of adjusting his collar. 'You must be told of our great mission. Without knowing that you will never understand why Ace is so necessary to our purpose.

'The Universe is old,' he began. 'The guardians of the cosmos, even the legendary Time Lords, Doctor, are long extinct. Only the Panjistri stand between the Universe and total destruction.

'Long, long ago, our scientists and philosophers realized that the Universe was on the point of collapse. Its energies had been used up, its expansion was complete. It had reached the limits of its growth. Like a piece of elastic all that was left to it was to contract, to fall back on to itself until it returned to the state it was when it first was born out of nothingness — a bright blazing pinprick of sheer energy.'

'Earth physicists called it the Big Crunch,' said the Doctor. 'A natural outcome of the Big Bang, when matter was first created and sent flying out into space.'

175

'But how are we and the Panjistri involved in this?' asked Arun.

'Before our world was destroyed in the solar flares, eighty-four of our race were selected to roam the Universe in Kandasi. Our mission was to scour what remained of creation, taking cells from every sentient species that still existed. All the knowledge, all the experience, all that was best in any race would then be inculcated into the most perfect race there had ever been, a species created by us.'

'And that's the Kirithons,' said Raphael. 'But how would that help stop the end of the Universe? And what has Ace got to do with it?'

'We culled the best of the Kirithons, the wisest, the most talented. Over nearly a thousand years we have distilled the best of the best into a vast machine, a bio-mechanism which, when completed, would become an independent life form, the only force capable of halting and reversing the destruction of the Universe.'

'But what sort of machine could do that?' asked Raphael.

'A life form that has reached the Omega Point,' the Doctor said darkly. 'An entity that has been everywhere, experienced every emotion, done everything, and knows all there has ever been to know – an omnipotent and omniscient being.'

'They're trying to create God?'

'A God machine, perhaps,' said the Doctor and turned back to Reptu. 'But why do you need Ace?'

Reptu allowed himself a wry laugh. 'The Kirithons we bred were too perfect, Doctor. We created them with every emotion but one. They lack a sense of aggression.'

'Hence your breeding of the Homunculus at the Harbours,' said the Doctor. 'A clumsy, bungled attempt to create a being of infinite aggression and violence.'

'That is correct, Doctor.'

'And now Ace, with her nitro-nine and all her frustrations, can provide that aggression.'

'Precisely, Doctor. When Ace's consciousness is absorbed into the heart of Kandasi then the God machine, as you call it, will be complete. Only then will the Universe be saved, only then will it be allowed to continue. Ace will die; but it is one life against billions.'

Raphael turned to the Doctor. 'You can't let them destroy Ace, Doctor,' he pleaded. 'There must be another way.'

The Doctor's voice was steady and hard. 'If it is a choice between Ace's future and the future of all creation, which would you choose?'

'I thought you said the Professor would be here,' said Ace as the Grand Matriarch led her into a large antiseptic room. A long couch and a bank of machinery dominated the room, which reminded Ace uncomfortably of a hospital operating room. A jewelled crown lay on an adjoining worktop.

'He will come,' the Matriarch assured her pleasantly. 'In the meantime please make yourself comfortable.'

'Look, I want to see the Professor now.' Ace turned around and headed for the door. 'If he's not here I'll look for him myself.'

The door slid firmly shut before her. Ace spun around to see the Matriarch advancing threateningly on her.

'You will be going nowhere at all, Earthchild,' she said in a guttural hiss. 'Your moment of apotheosis is arrived. It is time to serve your great destiny.'

Ace began to struggle as the Matriarch grabbed her arms, her long fingers cutting deep into her flesh. The frail old woman seemed to be possessed of some demonic force, so strong had she become.

A quick chop to the neck knocked Ace unconscious. Picking her up as easily as one would a baby, the Grand

177

Matriarch carried her over to the couch. The Earthchild's primitive body would have to be prepared before its unthinking aggression and independence of spirit could be absorbed into the God machine.

Then, when the Omega Point was reached, she would have mastery over all time, over all that was, is, and would be. The Grand Matriarch, she who had once been Lilith, laughed out loud.

For all she cared, the Universe and the Panjistri could then go and rot.

'Please believe me, Reptu,' pleaded the Doctor. 'You must release Ace now, and stop your misguided scheme!'

'Would you have billions die?'

'You stupid, stupid old man!' he blazed and clenched his fists in frustration. 'Everything must at some time die. It's part of the natural order of things. You cannot prolong life indefinitely; nothing was ever meant to live forever. Even the Universe must at some point cease to be and make way for something else.'

'You wish to be the hangman of all creation, Doctor?'

'Don't be so dramatic! This Universe still has ten billion years left to it, before entropy takes it over completely,' he insisted. 'And what you're creating at the heart of Kandasi is not going to reverse that. You are creating a monster, Reptu, a savage, vengeful, greedy monster!'

'The Grand Matriarch has —'

'The Grand Matriarch is not who you think she is and has never been so for five thousand years!' cried the Doctor.

For a second Reptu hesitated. 'What do you mean?' There was the slightest touch of doubt in his voice.

'It's what I've known all along, but was too proud to admit to myself,' he said. There was anguish and despair in the Doctor's face.

178

'Aeons ago — aeons in your past — I saved a new-born civilization from destruction. But in doing so I allowed the alien invader into my TARDIS, and the creature learnt to read the lines of time. I tried to destroy it, but the winds of the Vortex failed to harm it. Instead it rode the tempest. I followed it for a short distance; lost its trail; found it again, and succeeded in dispersing it.'

'But this being was not destroyed?' Reptu could not help being intrigued.

'No. I knew it would re-form. But I assumed it would be weak, that the next time I found it I would be able to finish it. I underestimated its cunning. It needed a breathing-space in which to recover its strength — and so it looked for a place to hide. I should have known it would have no respect for the laws of time. It hid in my own past.'

The Doctor took a deep, shuddering breath and continued.

'What my TARDIS knows, the Timewyrm knows. It disappeared into my past, choosing a moment when I was at my weakest. Unwittingly I sheltered it while bit by bit it rebuilt itself. It took the TARDIS to a distant planet where I met a small girl, a small girl whose skills of telepathy were so acute that she was the perfect host. Her name was Lilith.'

Reptu's lip trembled as the Doctor continued his story.

'Then it left me and like a horrible disease took over the body of that poor innocent girl. In time she became the Grand Matriarch, the leader of her people's quest to save the Universe.

'But you and the rest of the Panjistri are all pawns in her plan. The Grand Matriarch wants to destroy the Universe, not save it. Once the God machine is complete she will have mastery over all creation. And the Timewyrm within her will have all of time and space to feast upon!'

179

Reptu stood silent for a moment, as though considering the Doctor's words. Then he said: 'Have you quite finished with your lies, Doctor?'

'It's the truth,' insisted the Doctor. 'I made the most appalling, shameful mistake and we must save Ace before it's too late!'

By his side Raphael shivered; it seemed to him that it was getting very cold.

Chapter 19

One by one the lights on Kandasi faded and went out. Machinery which had functioned faultlessly for centuries whirred to a final irrevocable halt. The pumps which recycled and purified the space station's atmosphere fell silent, and the temperature began to drop.

The Doctor looked knowingly at Reptu. 'Now do you believe me?' he said wearily.

'But this is impossible,' Reptu said. 'Kandasi cannot shut down like this. Every function on board the station is controlled through the mind of the Matriarch. She would never allow this . . .'

'She has Ace now,' said the Doctor coldly. 'She no longer needs the Panjistri.'

'How long do we have before the life-support systems give out totally?' asked Arun urgently.

'Several hours,' answered Reptu. 'The automatic backup systems will give support for a further few hours, but then Kandasi will die.'

'So where is Ace?' demanded Raphael.

'Her primitive mind will have to be treated before it can be absorbed,' said Reptu. 'The Matriarch will have taken her to the centre of Kandasi.'

How do we get there?' asked the Doctor.

'Follow me.'

Ace's eyes snapped open and she tried to rise from the table. A flash of panic shot through her as she realized that her limbs would not obey her commands. Electrodes were taped to her forehead and wires led to a bank of machinery suspended directly above her. She turned her eyes to the Grand Matriarch, who sat calmly in her chair, gazing at her.

'Why can't I move?' Ace croaked.

'You are a prisoner of my will,' the Matriarch explained. 'Long ago, my people were accomplished telepaths and mind manipulators. Over the centuries our powers diminished. But for five thousand years I nurtured my talents for this one moment, when the Doctor would arrive here with his companion.'

'You've waited for me?'

'Or any of that warrior species the Doctor favours so much,' said the Matriarch and rose to walk over to Ace. 'But you were the one I hoped for. I have wanted you for such a long, long time.'

Ace was filled with cold horror as the Matriarch stroked her face, but she was powerless to resist. 'You, my dear, are the prize, so full of powerful emotion that you are like a tinderbox ready to explode.'

There was an almost lecherous look on the old woman's face; Ace trembled with disgust.

An unexpressed feeling of fear and panic permeated Kandasi, as Reptu led the Doctor, Raphael and Arun down to the centre of the space station. As they travelled deeper and deeper in a series of high-speed lifts, members of the Panjistri, their work forgotten, would look at them, pleading for reassurance.

182

Just as the Kirithons had depended on the Panjistri, so the Panjistri had depended for their wellbeing on the Grand Matriarch. Now that Kandasi was shutting down, now that their lifelong task was at its end and the Matriarch had apparently deserted them, they no longer had any sense of purpose. Their lives had suddenly become frighteningly empty.

'Haven't they minds of their own?' asked Arun contemptuously.

'They never really needed them before,' remarked the Doctor, as the doors of the lift opened.

'This is the lowermost deck,' said Reptu. 'We're two miles below the "surface" of Kandasi. Below us there is only the God machine, as you call it.'

'And this is where we can find Ace?' asked Raphael.

Reptu nodded. 'The Matriarch will have brought her to the Preparation Room. It was easy to drain the minds of Kirithons who were bred for that purpose. Earth people are much more difficult.'

'Yes, they're an infuriatingly imperfect species,' the Doctor said meaningfully. 'You could learn a lot from them. Now let's get to Ace; there's little time left.'

Reptu led them hurriedly through a series of winding corridors, all curiously still and empty. As they ran on their bodies seemed to grow heavier and it became increasingly difficult to move; it felt like wading through treacle.

'She's put up a gravity field,' cried the Doctor. 'We must concentrate. Try and break through it.'

For long agonizing minutes they pushed through the waves of energy which threatened to knock and crush them to the ground. The Doctor and Raphael took the lead but eventually even they had to give up as the Grand Matriarch's invisible defence became an impenetrable barrier.

They collapsed, exhausted, onto the ground.

'It's no good,' came a sad, lonely voice. 'I tried and she won't let even me in.'

'Fetch, what are you doing here?' asked Reptu as the Companion appeared.

'My mistress is sick; she needs my help.'

'Fetch, we have to get in there,' said the Doctor when Reptu had introduced them. 'Is there any way you can help us? Is there any other way into the Preparation Room?'

Fetch paused for thought, thinking back on the confidences the Matriarch had made to him over the past fifty years. 'There's a personal passage leading to it from her chambers.'

'Then can't we use that?' asked Raphael.

'My mistress has protected her chambers with the force field too.'

'There is one other way we could get there though,' said the Doctor, 'one place she wouldn't have thought of putting out a gravity field . . .'

The others looked at him blankly. 'Fetch, you must lead me to the Matriarch's apartments,' he said, suddenly taking charge. 'Reptu and Arun, you must gather together all the Panjistri. Bring them down here. A combination of their telepathic powers might just be able to break through her force field.'

'The Panjistri are responsible for what I am,' protested Arun. 'I cannot join with them.'

'Just do it!' barked the Doctor. 'You can solve your quarrels afterwards!'

'And what should I do, Doctor?' asked Raphael.

For a moment the Doctor coloured, and he hesitated. Then he said: 'Stay here, Raphael. Keep a watch until the others arrive. If there's any change in the situation, let us know.'

'But I want to do more!' he protested.

'I care about Ace as much as you do!' the Doctor snapped back, and then softened. 'Trust me, Raphael. Though I fear nothing short of a miracle could help us now,' he muttered, not quite under his breath.

As he turned to leave, an awkward glance passed between the Doctor and Raphael. Fetch tugged at the Doctor's sleeve.

'Doctor,' he said, 'promise me that whatever happens my mistress will not be harmed.'

'I promise, Fetch,' the Doctor said, and cursed himself for telling yet one more lie.

While Reptu and Arun gathered the Panjistri together, the Doctor and Fetch examined the entrance to the Matriarch's chambers. As Fetch had said, it was protected by an impenetrable force field.

The Doctor's plan was to reach the apartments from outside the space station. Using special blasting equipment, kept by the Panjistri for engineering work, he'd be able to cut through the porthole of the Matriarch's chamber. Once inside, Kandasi's defence circuits, now under some control by the Panjistri telepaths, should repair the breach and allow them access to the Matriarch's private route. It was, the Doctor insisted, not particularly convincingly, a simple operation.

No amount of argument on Fetch's part would dissuade him from accompanying the Doctor. If his mistress was in any trouble whatsoever he belonged by her side.

It took several minutes for the tall Panjistri to find spacesuits to fit the diminutive forms of the Doctor and Fetch. Even so the suits were ill-fitting; the Doctor only hoped that they wouldn't hinder their progress in the five-minute journey across the space station's hull.

The airlock door opened, and the Doctor and Fetch gently pushed themselves out into the void and began edging their way slowly along the hull of the space station to the Grand Matriarch's chamber. Their breathing echoed eerily across the radio link into each other's helmets.

Thousands of miles below them the tiny world of Kirith spun against a backdrop of stars. The Doctor paused to marvel at a sight which never failed to impress even after all these years: the infinite, vast unknown regions of space. Miríl should be here now, he thought sadly. This was his dream.

At the same time, small crablike robots, specially created by the Panjistri for outside maintenance work on Kandasi, activated themselves.

Their sensors had detected the Doctor and Fetch. Identifying them as space detritus, they now proceeded with their task of tracking down the waste material and disposing of it.

Raphael sat staring at the door of the Preparation Room. He shuddered to think what might be happening to Ace. She lay beyond that door, only a few feet away from him, and yet he was powerless to help her.

He stood up and walked forward. The force field still stood in his way; in a futile gesture he bashed his fists angrily against the invisible wall. And then he shivered.

He could hear a sound coming from somewhere far away. He looked around, thinking that Reptu and the other Panjistri were returning; but there was no sign of them.

No, it's not just a sound, he thought. It's music . . . it's a *koríntol* . . .

He frowned, wondering where the music was coming from. Then its tone changed to a harsher, sharper sound, almost like a voice, almost a voice calling out his name.

Ra-pha-el . . . Ra-pha-el . . .

He stepped towards the direction of the voice; and then he stopped and looked back at the door to the Preparation

186

Room. Ace was behind there; he should stay.

But there was nothing he could do for her there.

Ra-pha-el . . . Ra-pha-el . . .

He looked back again, sick with indecision. There is nothing I can do for you here, he repeated to himself. Something seemed to be tugging him forward. He felt an awful yawning pit in his stomach, and was surprised suddenly to find that he was trembling uncontrollably.

Then he was aware of moving forward, or rather of being moved forward, for he had made no conscious decision. And yet he didn't resist; it somehow seemed the right thing to do.

The music from the *koríntol* played louder and louder in his mind until its rhythms became the beating of his own two hearts.

And he was humming along with the music.

One of the hunter crabs scuttled soundlessly behind Fetch and, faster than the speed of thought, lashed out at him with a steel cable. The cable snaked and twisted around his foot, yanking him off the hull and sending him careering off into the blackness of space.

Alerted by his cries over the radio link, the Doctor spun around, almost losing his balance, to see two more crabs advancing towards him. Proboscises extended from their metal shells and spat beams of energy at him.

The Doctor darted out of their line of fire, but the sudden motion meant that he lost his grip on the hull. Like Fetch, he fell tumbling off into the void.

The Grand Matriarch looked down with an almost sexual delight as her machines probed and prepared Ace's mind for absorption into the God machine. She was at one with the machines as they fed on the violent side of Ace's character like filthy leeches, sucking on all the dark

187

emotions she preferred not to be reminded of.

They burned down Manisha's home, called her a filthy Paki. I want to kill those bastards, but that'd be too good for scum like that.

That thing at the Harbours; it was horrible and obscene. I was glad when it died.

I firebombed that old house. It was evil, it deserved it. Saw the flames lick around it, like flowers; I enjoyed that.

I trusted Mike, thought he was different from everyone else. Then he did the dirty on me. Just like the rest of them. Probably got what he deserved. Even Sorin died. I hate being out of control like that.

Karra is calling. The hunt. Smell the blood on the wind. Run.

Too frightened to move a muscle as the knife descends. Cold metal, sharp against my throat. The shame of fainting.

The Professor — Doctor. What's his game? How much does he really know? Just how safe is it travelling with him? Can he be trusted?

As the Grand Matriarch experienced the wonderful rush of Ace's hidden aggressions and fears, her whole body quaked with anticipation. Her fists clenched and unclenched greedily.

Her apotheosis was but minutes away.

Whirling deeper into space, away from the space station, the Doctor aimed the blasting equipment away from him towards the brown sphere of Kirith. Turning his head slowly around, he located Fetch twenty feet away from him. Silently he mouthed an old Gallifreyan charm; it would take pinpoint accuracy and a steady finger to achieve his plan.

A sharp short flick on the blaster sent a stream of energy away from the Doctor, propelling him towards the flailing body of Fetch. The Doctor collided with Fetch and the added momentum sent them flying away from the space station even faster.

Inside his helmet Fetch yelped with dismay as they spun further and further away from Kandasi.

'Trust me, Fetch,' said the Doctor, 'I know what I'm doing.' I think, he added silently.

Calmly he turned the blaster away and increased the power, propelling both of them back towards the shining white globe of the space station.

As Kandasi grew bigger and bigger, the Doctor repositioned the blaster. If he didn't fire it at precisely the right time and at the right power, they would be smashed to a pulp against the ship's side.

Chapter 20

Deeper and deeper Raphael descended, drifting in a daze like a sleepwalker. He was vaguely aware of doors opening of their own accord, but he was more concerned with the strange noises which echoed through his brain.

Through misted eyes he saw pumps glowing and pulsing with eerie blue lights; he was aware of stepping through dense jungles of glittering wires and cables. As he brushed the gossamer threads aside, his fingers tingled as they charged his body with electrical and psychic pulses.

He went further down and the air seemed to become thicker, almost tangible. It cut painfully into his lungs, making him gasp.

A final pair of doors opened. As fierce white light rushed out of the open doorway, almost blinding him with its brilliance, Raphael's mind finally cleared and at last he understood.

He was standing on a platform overlooking a vast arena, gazing down into the very centre of Kandasi. There, suspended in black space tens of miles below, hung the machine around which the entire space station had been built.

It was a golden sphere, several miles in diameter,

featureless and perfect. All about it beams of light swept and danced, some supporting it in the void, others feeding it with raw untamed energy.

Raphael felt its cold hard presence: the God machine. The thing that has been everywhere and has done everything, that knows all and needs nothing.

As he looked deep into its brilliant surface he seemed to see a million different faces, the images and the memories of all those the Panjistri had culled throughout the years, twinkling as the stars might have done when the Universe was still in its infancy.

And somewhere in the depths of that perfect sphere, he seemed to see his parents, and his best friend, and Darien's sister Kareena, and all the others bred and killed so that the Timewyrm might have dominion over all creation.

And then those images coalesced until they became one image, or rather the suggestion of an image.

And whether he saw himself in that light, or Ace, or the Doctor, or Miríl, he was never completely sure.

Chapter 21

At last you have arrived, and my becoming is complete.

– Was I expected then?

– You were ... invited. You have become the part that I was lacking, the part that I cannot control. Without you it was becoming a little too boring in here.

– What are you?

– What do you want me to be? I'm whatever you want to make of me. Everything you have always wanted to be.

– And you've been waiting for me forever?

– Not you as you were. But you as you have become. Yes, I've been waiting for that forever ...

– But someone else was responsible for that.

– No matter. She was the catalyst, but the questions and the emotions were always within you ... Now, do you/we accept and embrace with understanding our apotheosis?

– Do I have a choice?

– Of course. We all of us have a choice. Even me.

– So what's in it for me?

– All that was, is and could be we would experience together.

– And beyond that?

– We choose not to go.
– I see I can't avoid it. But will it be fun?
– It's what you make of it. But it could be an awfully big adventure, Raphael ...

In a shower of splinters of plastic and fire, the Doctor and Fetch burst into the chambers of the Grand Matriarch. As the pressure destabilized they dived to the floor.

Long seconds passed before Kandasi reacted and rearranged its structure to seal the window. As the pressure stabilized and oxygen was pumped back into the room the Doctor helped Fetch to his feet. Fetch took off his helmet and began to unzip his spacesuit. The Doctor stopped him.

'There's no time for that,' he said impatiently. 'Where's the way to the Preparation Room?'

'This way, Doctor,' he said and opened a door leading to a private lift.

The Grand Matriarch's fingers lighted gently, reverentially, on the helmet which awaited its final victim. Once placed on Ace's head it would sap away her aggressive tendencies and transfer them directly into the heart of the God machine. Like a holy man carrying a sacred relic, she glided stately over to the defenceless Ace.

She stiffened when the door to the elevator whooshed open. As the Doctor and Fetch raced into the room she bared her teeth in a grimace of hate, like a snake confronting its prey.

'Matriarch! Don't!' screamed the Doctor.

'Doctor –' she hissed the word – 'after all this time, we meet again!'

The Doctor stopped, suddenly shocked beyond measure at the sight of the little smiling girl he had once known, now changed into a twisted, perverted, lusting harpy. And he hung his head, recognizing the role he had played in

193

her transformation; if only he hadn't been so supremely confident of his abilities all those years ago.

'Matriarch, I beg of you. You don't understand what you're doing,' he pleaded. 'There's still time to exorcize the evil which has possessed you.'

The Matriarch snarled in reply.

'Then take me instead,' he offered. 'Only spare Ace's life.'

'No, Professor!' cried Ace.

The Matriarch ignored her outburst. 'Do you take me for a simpleton, Doctor? A mind as dark and devious as yours, absorbed into my machine? That would not serve my purposes.'

'Matriarch – Lilith. Please.'

The Grand Matriarch flung her head back and laughed triumphantly.

'Then you leave me no alternative,' said the Doctor grimly and raised the blaster, directing it at the Matriarch.

'The man of peace at last resorts to violence,' chuckled the Grand Matriarch.

Her green eyes blazed and the gun vanished from the Doctor's hands. 'I already have great powers, Time Lord. Soon my abilities will be without bound. Now kneel – kneel and pay me homage.'

The Doctor grimaced as he fought the huge mental powers of the Grand Matriarch, augmented by her union with the Timewyrm. Slowly, inexorably he found himself being pushed to his knees by the sheer force of her possessed will. Ace looked on in horror.

'Mistress,' said Fetch. 'I don't understand. Please, let me help you . . .'

The Matriarch looked wearily at the Companion who had served her faithfully and without question for fifty years. 'You again? If you only knew how you bored me with your snivelling and crawling. You are no better than

194

the irradiated cells you and your kind were first created from.'

'Mistress?' There was a wealth of emotion in that one word. The Matriarch's eyes flashed once more and Fetch stiffened and fell down dead.

'You callous bitch!' cried Ace. 'He loved you!'

'Always so aggressive, *Dorothy*,' said the Matriarch, and Ace growled in anger at hearing her hated real name. 'It's time to put that aggression to good use.'

Still on his knees, the Doctor watched in horror as the Grand Matriarch, she who was once Lilith and was now possessed by the Timewyrm, raised the crown high above Ace's head.

'Now let all of time be mine to feast upon,' exulted the Matriarch and brought the crown down.

Suddenly the doors burst open, and a bitterly cold wind swept through the room. The metal walls buckled and collapsed, crashing down on the prone body of Fetch. The Matriarch screamed in horror as the helmet crashed to the ground, smashing into a thousand glittering pieces. Her mental control broken, the Doctor sprang to his feet and rushed over to the dazed Ace, helping her off the couch.

Beyond the Preparation Room, in the rest of Kandasi, machines exploded or burst into flame. The Panjistri and their Companions ran in blind terror as the floor shook and then exploded beneath their feet.

In some parts of the space station metal walls turned to molten metal within minutes; in other parts the air itself froze solid. Objects which were not bolted to the floor began to rise of their own accord and smash helplessly into each other.

Viewports smashed outwards, exposing whole sections of the space station to the airlessness and sub-zero temperatures of the vacuum. Throughout the ship alarms blared and emergency units went into action trying in vain

195

to limit the damage.

Kandasi trembled and shook in its orbit.

'Professor, what's happening?'

'The Grand Matriarch — follow her!'

White with terror, the Grand Matriarch had hitched up her skirts and with her new-found vigour was running desperately down to the centre of Kandasi. Dodging falling structures, the Doctor and Ace followed her. The ground cracked and rocked sickeningly beneath their feet.

As they ran things started to stabilize and quieten down, as though whatever power had been unleashed was now learning how to control and regulate itself. By the time they had reached the Matriarch, on the balcony overlooking the God machine, only a distant rumbling suggested that anything was amiss.

The Matriarch spun round when they approached her. Silhouetted in the golden glow she seemed like a demon bathing in the flames of hell.

'Professor, what's happened?' asked Ace breathlessly.

'The God machine's out of her control now,' he said softly and put an arm around Ace's shoulder.

Ace felt her body tense. 'Raphael . . .?'

'He's learning to take control of it, become part of it . . .'

'Five thousand years of waiting,' wailed the Matriarch, 'to be thwarted at the moment of success.'

The Doctor looked at the figure of the Grand Matriarch of the Panjistri with genuine compassion.

Convulsions racked her entire body, and the Doctor and Ace watched in horror as a hideous form began to disassociate itself from its reluctant host. The Timewyrm, translucent and glowing red with hatred, stood staring at the Doctor. Little remained now of the goddess it had once been. Its body was metallic and serpentine, its face a contorted mask of loathing. It took a step forward.

The whole chamber was suddenly bathed in a brilliant

light, and the Doctor and Ace instinctively covered their eyes. The only sounds to be heard were the bloodcurdling wails and sub-animal screeches of the Timewyrm in its final unremitting agonies.

When the light dimmed and they could see again, only the Grand Matriarch remained on the gallery. The Timewyrm had vanished, removed by that part of what had been Raphael which now controlled the God machine.

For a second, deprived of the power of the Timewyrm, the Grand Matriarch appeared her true age, a withered crone, thousands of years past her time of dying. Her headdress fell off, revealing a bald, mottled skull. The fire in her eyes had died and they darted blindly about. Her brittle bones, unable to support her weight, snapped under her and she slumped to the floor.

She tried to drag herself forward on withered broken arms towards the Doctor, who turned his face away in shameful revulsion. Her cracked lips opened, but the only sound that came out of them was a dry plaintive squeak.

And then she was suffused in a blissful orange light. The Doctor and Ace looked on in wonder at the pathetic old hag before them.

Time seemed to be folding back on itself. The flesh, taut over her cheekbones, became fresh and supple once more. Hair began to grow rapidly on her skull, at first white, then grey, and then a wonderful flaming red.

Further back in time she regressed until she was a child again, a beautiful innocent red-haired girl. She smiled, her first smile in over five thousand years, and looked at the Doctor. 'I like you, sir; you're nice.'

The Doctor shuddered.

It was as a child, cleansed of all guilt and her burden at long last lifted, that the Grand Matriarch died.

An hour later Ace stared accusingly at the Doctor. There

197

were unshed tears in her eyes.

'You knew, didn't you? You knew all along.'

The Doctor didn't answer. He laid a hand on Ace's shoulder; she pushed him away. 'Leave me alone,' she snapped. 'It's because of you that Raphael's dead.'

'Ace, there was no other way. Please believe me,' he begged. 'It was Raphael's own decision. If I could have saved his life I would have done. But it was either him − or the end of everything.'

'I could have gone.'

'No no no,' he said emphatically. 'You're too aggressive, too full of grudges and frustrations. It was exactly what the Timewyrm wanted.'

She turned her face away. 'You could have gone,' she said in a monotone.

'You don't understand, Ace,' he said tearfully. 'Once it possessed my mind the Timewyrm would have used me just as it did before. I'm no innocent, Ace.'

'No, you're not, are you?' Ace bit her lip. 'Why don't you trust us? Why do you watch us suffer, and manipulate us like some ... Why do you do it when you know all along what's going to happen?'

The Doctor shook his head. 'We all of us have free choice, Ace. And Raphael made his.' He forced her to look at him. 'What Raphael did wasn't to save the Universe or even to defeat the Timewyrm. He sacrificed himself for you, for that rebel from Perivale with all her faults and imperfections who was always out to prove herself. He loved you so much that he gave his life for you. And that's something that will always be with you.'

Ace attempted a smile. 'He said he needed me. It's nice to be needed.'

'It is,' he agreed, but Ace wasn't too sure whether he meant it.

Arun interrupted them. 'Doctor, Ace, the transporter

room has switched itself on . . .'

The Doctor chuckled. 'I rather think we're being told to go home,' he said. 'Are Reptu and the Panjistri waiting there?'

Arun nodded.

'Well then, my friend, lead the way!'

The Doctor took Ace's arm. He looked around at the devastation of Kandasi, thought of the lives that had been lost both here and on Kirith. If only there had been another way. There was a sad knowing gleam in his eyes.

'In the mythology of your planet, Ace, Raphael was one of the angels of God. It's rather appropriate, I think.'

Sadly they turned away and made their way back down to Kirith.

Epilogue

The Doctor and Ace watched on the TARDIS scanner screen as Kandasi exploded in a blinding kaleidoscope of colour. For a moment an unearthly glow hung in the sky and then that too dispersed.

The Doctor smiled. 'At least Raphael's got his dream now,' he said.

'What do you mean?'

The Doctor adjusted the scanner controls; a vast star field appeared on the screen. 'He's out there now, somewhere among the stars. Perhaps he can carry Miríl's dream with him.'

'And the Universe is safe?'

'It's still got a few billion years left to it,' he said casually. 'And then it will end, its purpose achieved, just as nature intended.'

'Which is?'

The Doctor tapped the side of his nose lightly. 'Aha ...'

'All right, so don't tell me.'

'I don't think the Panjistri will try their little game again.'

'And Kirith?'

'The Panjistri are falling over themselves to be helpful.

Wonderful what a bit of forced coexistence will do to even the most conceited of people.'

Ace agreed, but she wasn't thinking of the Panjistri.

'Reptu has promised to cure Arun's people.' And Revna's regime was based on fear and ignorance; in the new circumstances she won't last long.'

'But how will the Kirithons take to the Panjistri?' asked Ace. 'After all they've done?'

'That's up to them; I think it's about time that they started looking after themselves, don't you? Make their own judgements for a change,' said the Doctor. 'I hate meddling at the best of times.'

Pull the other one, Professor! she thought.

'You know,' the Doctor mused aloud as he prepared the TARDIS for take-off, 'a being like Raphael wandering around the Universe might not be all that bad. The old place could do with regaining some of its lost innocence — '

'Professor, look!'

'What is it?'

Ace pointed to the counter on the control console which was supposed to register the existence of the Timewyrm. It was emitting a regular but very faint flashing light.

The Doctor checked the controls urgently. They were all functioning normally.

'I don't understand,' he said. 'Raphael destroyed the Timewyrm.'

'Professor, I don't think he did.'

'What do you mean?'

'He hated killing,' she said, remembering the Harbours. 'He was devastated when he killed the Homunculus.'

The Doctor felt his two hearts pounding with dread. 'So he didn't destroy it after all; he only banished it.' He looked at the countless stars displayed on the scanner screen.

'It's out there somewhere, waiting for us.'